The Colour of The Young

by
Cornelius Rainsford

Grosvenor House
Publishing Limited

All rights reserved
Copyright © Cornelius Rainsford, 2011

Cornelius Rainsford is hereby identified as author of this
work in accordance with Section 77 of the Copyright, Designs
and Patents Act 1988

The book cover picture is copyright to Inmagine Corp LLC

This book is published by
Grosvenor House Publishing Ltd
28-30 High Street, Guildford, Surrey, GU1 3HY.
www.grosvenorhousepublishing.co.uk

This book is sold subject to the conditions that it shall not, by way of
trade or otherwise, be lent, resold, hired out or otherwise circulated
without the author's or publisher's prior consent in any form of binding or
cover other than that in which it is published and
without a similar condition including this condition being imposed
on the subsequent purchaser.

A CIP record for this book
is available from the British Library

ISBN 978-1-907652-97-4

Also by this author

Tadlers Warren (Book 1)
The Beggar's Bowl (Book 1)
666 and a 9millimetre
Murder in the Rain

Dedication

To my lovely wife Joan, and even our wonderful cat Oscar, who more than once, tiddled on my precious manuscript pages, despite having two litter trays and being allowed to sleep in my favourite armchair.

CHAPTER ONE

Saturday 5th June 2010

Maggie Pemberton let herself into the five bedroom, Georgian-style semi in Hampstead that she shared with her husband John.

The two bags of Tesco shopping she carried were heavy, and as she struggled along the hall to the kitchen, she glanced through the living-room door on her left, where John was sitting in his favourite armchair, watching the highlights of the football played earlier in the day.

She could just see his head of greying hair sticking above the back of the chair, and she smiled. John was very tall *'Six feet five and a big bit,'* as he liked to say. For, it seemed to Maggie that her husband was six feet five of legs, and all that was left for his body was the bit. Because, when she sat next to him they were practically the same height, despite her being only five feet four.

Her pet name for him was Spiderman. He loved the name, and whenever she used it he always responded by telling her that she was his little Fly Girl, who had flown into his web very nicely indeed, and that there was no escape.

Maggie left her husband to his football and entered the large, designer kitchen. Each time she came through the kitchen door, she felt a touch of disappointment as well as pleasure at what she saw. Thirty-nine thousand pounds was the price tag for this envy of the neighbourhood. *'And worth every, hard-earned penny,'* John would declare whenever some unfortunate was foolish enough to suggest that there may have been just a smidgen of over-indulgence. The perpetrator of the unjust criticism was then usually subjected to a detailed description of this culinary palace, that sometimes lasted a full hour; unless Maggie was there to intervene in this verbal equivalent of a cat-o-nine tails flogging, and rescued the victim with the offer of a cup of tea and a chat in the living-room. She never could stand cruelty of any kind.

Maggie liked the kitchen her husband had designed for her, well enough: after all, it was spacious, and beautiful in its own way. And the cost hadn't been an issue, because, although not exactly affluent, they were comfortably off. However, it had to be said, and she would never tell John this as it would certainly upset him, that she didn't exactly need the double-fronted stainless steel oven, the twenty foot long black marble worktop that had been flown in from Italy, the cupboards made from a rare, African hardwood, the huge, American fridge-freezer that bleeped whenever its internal temperature exceeded a predetermined setting, the double, Belfast sink with gold taps, and the early Victorian, Italian-style, handmade floor tiles that, in their previous existence, adorned the great entrance hall of a stately home.

    The less extravagant truth of it for her was, that deep in her heart where John's wishes held no dominion, she longed for the cosy and simple little kitchen in her grandmother's cottage, where she was taught how to bake the perfect bread-and-butter pudding, and scones that were so light they could rival the finest soufflé. And it wasn't as if her husband was an aspiring Gary Rhodes, unable to create his masterpieces in anything less than an inspirational kitchen.

A week previously she had returned from a shopping trip to find the saucepan of milk for his drinking chocolate overflowing, the stirring spoon on the floor and chocolate powder scattered all over the worktop.

"Do you want any help, dear?" Maggie had asked, trying to keep a straight face as John whipped the saucepan from the hob, spilling even more of the milk.

"Bloody, over-complicated thing!" John snapped, throwing the saucepan into the sink before storming out of the kitchen with long strides and a red face.

Much to his annoyance John's face always flushed tomato-red when he felt he had made a complete fool of himself.

Of course, he always claimed it was red from anger, but Maggie knew it was embarrassment that prompted one of her husband's more endearing vulnerabilities. He was red-faced when he first asked her out, and when he asked her to marry him. It was simply his way and she loved him for it.

Clearly, the best thing about an expensive kitchen for John Pemberton was its price, Maggie concluded. And in time she would no doubt forget that tiny little place in her grandmother's cottage, where food was created with love as the main ingredient. But for now she would have to console herself with the fact that in such a big house as theirs, a tiny cottage kitchen would look very much out of place, and perhaps even a bit silly.

As Maggie put her shopping away, John walked into the kitchen with that casual style that always reminded her of a fast-gun marshal in the old west, patrolling the streets of his town.

She loved westerns ever since she was a little girl. They had such a sense of simple justice and morality about them; not like the films of today where the good guy ends up as the bad guy more often than not. At least that would never happen to John. He would always be on the side of right, no matter what the situation.

John caught the tiny smile that appeared on his wife's lips as he filled a glass with cold water from the tap at the sink. He downed the liquid in one, long swallow and stared fixedly at her.

"Help yourself to another shot of rotgut whisky, mister," Maggie quipped with a laugh.

John grinned. "You and your westerns, love. I sometimes wonder if you wouldn't have been better off being born in the old Wild West, and hitching yourself up to some fancy, town official."

"Maybe I have found myself a twenty-first century one, pardner," said Maggie.

"Could be, pardner," said John in an exaggerated, American drawl. "Now, how's about some victuals woman, and nothing too heavy for me tonight. Mind you, I ain't fixin to eat no more of those darn beans-on-toast of yours, or the cat, if we had one, would probably vamoose to the hills for some fresh air."

"Then how's about a ham-and-tomato sandwich?" Maggie offered.

"I reckon that'll do just fine," said John. Then he leaned against the sink and observed his wife as she set about preparing the food. It always amazed him how she managed to retain her slim, youthful figure without any apparent effort. She had never been on a diet since they got married nearly forty years ago. And as far as he could tell, she ate whatever she wanted. She even enjoyed a glass of red wine with her dinner most evenings. He wondered for a long time where all the calories went, until it came to him one day. Maggie Pemberton used up her excess calories in her laughter. How she loved to laugh; at funny things, and even at sad films because of the silly way they made her cry.

Maggie wasn't exactly beautiful; John had never thought she was. But she was certainly pretty; just like a daisy. Her face was round and a little on the full side. Her eyes were large and blue. Her lips were thin and her hair, once mouse-brown, was now turning grey. Maggie Pemberton could be described in the way a film critic once said of Robert Mitchum 'Take any one of his features and there is nothing special about it. However, put them all together and strangely enough you have a pretty good-looking face.'

John once told her she looked like a younger Judy Dench, and she was flattered, much to his relief, because Maggie could sulk for England, and Europe as well, when she was upset.

"Jennifer and Peter are coming round for dinner on Monday afternoon," said Maggie, buttering four slices of bread.

"Are they bringing James and Katherine?" John asked, pleased by the news.

Maggie shook her head. "Not this time, dear. Jennifer said it takes ages to settle them after one of their visits here. All they want to do when they get home is play the games you played with them, and she's just too tired these days."

"You should never be too tired to play with your children," said John firmly, filling his glass once more.

"Easy for you to say," Maggie replied. "You don't have a high-powered job to go to five days a week, and a slave-driver for a boss."

John pulled a sour face. "Don't get me started on that particular subject. You know how I feel about the whole, ridiculous situation. Working herself to death for that law firm isn't going to do her, or her family any good in the end."

Maggie added slices of tomato and ham to the bread. "She wants to be a barrister, John. You know how these things go. The way to the top is work, work, work, and nothing else will do. Sacrifices made now will reap dividends later on; you'll see."

"And probably make strangers of her children in the process," John growled. "Anyway, Peter agrees with me, and he should know better than anyone."

"Not the same thing at all," said Maggie. "Peter wanted to be a professional footballer long before he married Jennifer. It was an injury that put an end to his dreams, not hard work. Anyway, he's a part-time coach now and loves every minute of it. So, in a way, all that training he did before his injury has stood him in good stead."

"That's as may be," said John. "But I can see the disappointment in his eyes when he plays football with James. He misses that dream of his far more than he will ever let on. I don't want that to happen to our only daughter. Surely you know there are nowhere near enough places for all of them. I knew someone at work who was a barrister for just two years before ending up as a cleaner."

Maggie frowned. "I remember you telling me about him before. Didn't he have some kind of breakdown?"

"Yes he did; but what do you think brought on that breakdown; pressure, that's what turned him from a highly functioning human being into a mop-and-bucket man, daydreaming his life away."

"From how you described him," said Maggie, handing her husband his sandwich, "I very much doubt it was pressure that brought down that poor man. I think it was his makeup; his lack of mental stamina, if you like. And don't you for one minute think that Jennifer is liable to go the same way. She can take all the pressure those wig-headed, pompous Etonians can throw at her, and dish out a little pressure of her own, if she needs to."

"So that's how you sum up our daughter, is it; hard-boiled and tough?" John declared, annoyed by his wife's persistence.

Maggie laughed. "Don't be so melodramatic, John, for Heaven's sake. You know very well that Jennifer is a loving, caring person, who would never dream of hurting anyone. Mind you, I think she would be rather flattered to hear that being said about her. She admires the Queen for the way she's handled all the problems that have plagued the Royal Family in recent years. You mark my words; one day the Queen will be sending for our Jen, and no one will be more proud than you when that day comes. Just think, dear; *Dame Jennifer Barclay*: it has such resonance to it; like poetry."

"What about our sons, love?" said John, still trying to win the argument. "What future does your crystal ball see for them?"

"The possibilities are, as they say, endless," Maggie replied, her tone more serious now. "Robert has his antiques business, and Mark, well, you know your youngest as well as I, dear. He doesn't stick with anything long enough to make an impression on it. I suppose he will settle down sooner or later. After all, he's nearly thirty years old and he can't stay single for the rest of his life; at least I hope he can't. More grandchildren would be nice."

"Is he still with the girl he met on that speed-dating thing?" John asked, silently conceding defeat.

"You mean Tracy? As far as I know he is. Mind you, I don't see any future for them. She's far too flighty. He's bound to see that eventually and find someone more suitable."

John suppressed a laugh. Maggie was touchy when it came to Mark, and discussing any topic concerning him was moving in dangerous territory.

"You're just looking to have two Dames in the family, love," he quipped. "Now wouldn't that give old Pokey-Nosey next door something to chew on."

"John!" Maggie exclaimed with a mixture of humour and disapproval. "Mrs Tatterly isn't nosey. She's just a bit lonely, that's all."

"Lonely!" John declared. "Within one week of us moving in here, she knew more about our family than I did. And do you know something, she even had the nerve to remind me that it was our thirtieth wedding anniversary, and she even told me to buy you a car to replace your old Vauxhall Astra."

"You did buy me a new car," said Maggie, "so her advice was good, wasn't it? I mean, I was delighted when I saw it parked in the drive."

"Yes," said John indignantly. "That's because the old biddy only reminded me just one day before our anniversary, and I didn't have time to think of getting you something else. If she was going to stick her nose into our business she should have done it properly and given me a week at least to buy you something; well, something less extravagant. She sent me into a right panic dropping it on me like that as I was leaving for work. I'm sure she did it deliberately, just because I accidentally stepped on her Choobywooby's paw the month before, and they say old people are forgetful. Well, I think she still broods about it today, even though the thing passed away from natural causes nearly eight years ago."

"Poor little thing," said Maggie, sympathetically. "When you walked on its paw I heard it screech from in here. You knew very well she was over-protective of that Chihuahua, and you should have watched where you were going. Anyway, if it wasn't for Pokey-Nosey, as you call her, you would still be sleeping on the settee. Now, I think I'll finish this sandwich in the living-room and have an early night. Oh, that mattress needs changing. Every time I turned over the last few nights, I thought that bumpy spring would snap. God knows where it could have ended up."

"You needn't worry, love," John quipped, a huge grin on his face, "no broken spring in its right mind would dare give you a prod."

"I'd rather not risk it, if you don't mind," Maggie replied. "It might turn out to be one of those radical springs. Anyway, first thing in the morning I'll phone Glackwells and order a new one."

John followed his wife into the living-room, eating his sandwich as he went. If truth be told, he was feeling rather tired himself. Retirement was turning out to be far more demanding than he expected. Maggie still had a whole list of jobs for him to do around the house, and if anything, the list was growing longer. Not that he minded. Maggie being a house-proud woman, and liked things perfect, although it was not quite an obsession with her, thank God. His shoes occasionally managed to escape from their designated resting position next to the hall table, although this freedom didn't usually last more than an hour or so. And sometimes his car keys were far from the hook on the living-room wall. However, when it came to papers and magazines, Maggie held them in a tight discipline that would be the envy of a Regimental Sergeant Major. Her motto was 'If they weren't being read, they had no right being seen.'

The few hours remaining before bed-time were spent watching television.

"That was a lovely programme about Southern Ireland," Maggie said with a sigh, turning off the television. "I suppose much of England was like that a few hundred years ago."

"Ireland is a modern country, too, love," said John. "And Dublin is one of the top cities in the world, from what I hear."

"I was referring to all those beautiful, open spaces, with stunning hills and wonderful lakes," Maggie chided. "Very much like Scotland is now, I suppose, but with so much more of it. I think it's a great shame that England has lost so many of its truly wild places."

"Plenty of National Parks in England," said John. "With lots of space to roam if you need to do that sort of thing."

"Course there are," said Maggie, "but those parks are so tidy and managed. Oh, I don't know; when that Irish presenter just now said that you could walk a whole day through many parts of Southern Ireland without even seeing another person, I was thinking how magical it must be: what did he call them *'The Spirit Gardens of Eire.'* In rare, wild places like that you could probably discover your soul."

"Steady on, love!" John laughed. "I'm perfectly happy living here in case you are having any funny ideas. And you do know, don't you, that the vast majority of the population live in Dublin. England would be like that too if everyone moved to London."

"I suppose so," Maggie admitted. "Mind you, the Irish people probably discovered their souls before they moved to Dublin."

"Oh, I see; so that's why there is so much open space, is it; because the Irish found their souls?" said John incredulously.

"Yes, dear," Maggie replied with a smile, "it is."

"Then why are so many English people still living in the countryside, may I inquire?" said John.

Maggie shrugged. "I don't know, dear. Perhaps English souls are a little harder to find, or they have forgotten how to look for them."

"Aaa, that's your Irish grandmother talking," John scoffed. "Remember, I met her just before she died. She could talk the hind leg off a donkey, given half a chance."

"An English donkey or an Irish donkey?" Maggie asked, suppressing a giggle.

"Well, it would have to be an English one," said John. "All the Irish donkeys are probably off roaming the wild places trying to find out if they have souls or not."

"Then I'm off to bed before we get into the subject of souls and animals," said Maggie, yawning. "Otherwise we could end up becoming vegetarians, and neither of us are that keen on vegetables. Are you coming up?"

"Be there later," said John. "I want to finish that novel if I can. Goodnight, love."

"Goodnight, dear," said Maggie, heading for the hall.

It was three minutes to twelve before John, struggling to stay the course reading a recommended but tedious story about a Russian spy, finally gave up and retired himself.

CHAPTER TWO

Sunday 6th June

Maggie came into the kitchen the following morning to find her husband sitting at their glass-top table. He was hunched over a cup of coffee, and didn't acknowledge her presence with anything more than a quick glance and a grunt.

She sat opposite him, feeling a touch of apprehension.

In the six months of their retirement, not once had he left their bed before her. No matter how late in the morning she got up, she always left him still asleep, except for this particular morning. It was strangely unnerving.

"Bad night, dear?" she asked in a soft tone.

John stared at her and she was shocked at what she saw. He seemed to have aged ten years overnight, and his lips were tight; as if clinched in anger.

"Depends on what you mean by bad," he muttered.

"Well, did you have a nightmare, or a restless night? Was it the mattress, because I'm going to buy a new one today?"

John returned his attention to the half-empty cup of coffee. He was holding a teaspoon in his right hand and began slowly stirring the liquid, as if enthralled by its movement as it began to spin inside the cup.

Maggie decided not to press her husband any further, and so she left the table to make herself a cup of tea.

When she returned to the table, John was still stirring his coffee.

"What's the matter, dear?" she implored, reaching across the table and touching his hand.

John stared at her again. There was an odd look in his eyes this time; a look signifying that a great change had taken place inside him.

"Are you happy, Maggie?" he asked in a low voice.

Maggie's heart missed a beat in fright. However, it was not the question itself that alarmed her, but how her husband had addressed her. She could remember every occasion he had used her first name when speaking to her. The first was fifteen years earlier when he told her he was having chest pains, the second was when he told her that the doctors had diagnosed meningitis as the cause of Mark's high temperature when he was twenty-two years old, and the last time was when he phoned her from the police station after getting into a serious fight in the pub. Now he was using it again and it instilled dread in her soul.

"Of course I'm happy, dear," she answered with a weak smile. "After all, you always said you could tell whether I was happy or not by the slices of tomato I placed on the bread when I was making sandwiches: thin slices meant all systems go, and thick slices meant head for the hills, buckos."

"I'm being serious!" John snapped, letting the spoon clatter in the cup.

Maggie struggled to contain her growing panic. "So am I, John. I have always been contented married to you. We have three healthy children, two beautiful grandchildren, and this house is everything I have ever wished for. Why wouldn't I be happy?"

"So you have no regrets; not a single one?" said John.

The question was aggressive, almost accusing.

Maggie hesitated. "Well, perhaps there are a few minor things; of course there are. After all, nothing in this life is perfect. But they don't concern our marriage, if that's what you mean?"

"What are these things?" said John, still sounding aggressive.

"I told you," Maggie replied with a hint of exasperation, "nothing serious. However, since it's obviously important that I provide you with a few details, I wish Mark was more like his sister, and -"

Her grandmother's kitchen suddenly popped into her head, but she suppressed it. Now was certainly not the time to discuss that particular topic. Perhaps one day, but not now.

"Go on," John prompted eagerly, "what else?"

Maggie shrugged. "Just a silly thing really. I've always wanted an apple tree. There used to be one in my grandmother's garden. The branches used to droop with the weight of the fruit during the good years and I used to love picking them with her. But I knew a tree like that would cast too much shade on your flowers in this small garden, so I kept it to myself."

John sagged in his chair, as if all the life had suddenly drained from his body. "That's not what I meant at all," he sighed with a shake of his head.

Maggie felt indignation despite the worry about her husband's behaviour. "Well, I did say there was nothing serious, so why insist on hearing them?"

John didn't answer. His attention was once more on his cooling cup of coffee.

"Look, dear," Maggie pleaded, "what's this all about? When you went to bed last night you were fine. Oh, I know you are disappointed in that book Andrew recommended, but surely you're not bothered that much about it?"

Then a frightening thought struck her and she paled. "You're not sick, are you? You haven't got those pains again? Please, John; answer me, for Heavens sake?"

"I'm not sick," John muttered. "It's nothing like that."

A sigh of relief escaped Maggie's lips, and she covered her face for a moment. Then she regained her composure and stared fixedly at her husband. "Look at me, dear!" she ordered.

John raised his eyes.

Maggie's expression became firm with resolve. "Now you listen to me, John Pemberton. We don't have secrets from one another in this marriage, and we're certainly not going to start now. To begin with you have a much better memory than I have and it wouldn't be fair; so out with it. Why are you at our breakfast table, doing your very best to drive me crazy with worry?"

"I had a dream, love," John said instantly. "Or, not a dream exactly; more like a vision, I suppose."

"I see," said Maggie, not sure what to see.

John then straightened up in his chair and new life seemed to flow into him. He pushed the coffee cup aside and placed his elbows on the table, leaning his body forwards. His eyes were glowing now, and his clasped hands began to unclasp and clasp again.

"Can I ask you something, love: it's very important?" he said.

Maggie's concern disappeared in an instant at the sound of her husband's usual name for her, and she felt that everything was going to be all right. "Of course you can, dear," she said, smiling and leaning across to touch his hands once more.

John seemed not to notice. "You know when you dream; I mean, when you've had one of those intense dreams that stay with you most of the next day? You know you were dreaming, don't you? I mean, when you wake up, you realize then that it was only a dream, no matter how vivid it was? Whereas, for instance, when you come down to the kitchen in the middle of the night for a glass of water, you know you're actually getting that glass of water, don't you, and not dreaming that you are getting the glass of water? I mean, there is a sense of reality about it; like we feel now; this minute. We both know, don't we; without a shred of doubt that we are here, having breakfast; not in bed dreaming we are?"

Maggie was confused. "I think I understand what you're saying, dear," she offered in a quiet voice. "So is that what happened to you last night? Did you have a vivid dream that's bothering you?"

John's face twisted in anger. "It wasn't a bloody dream, Maggie!" he retorted. "That's what I'm trying to tell you. Haven't you been listening to me?"

Startled by the rebuke, Maggie struggled to compose herself. "Of course I've been listening, John, but I have to say you're not making much sense. If you didn't have a dream, then why did you go on about one just now?"

"Because I'm trying to make you understand that I didn't have a dream; that it was something far more real; more important."

"All right then," said Maggie, trying to sound matter-of-fact, "you weren't dreaming last night. Something obviously happened, so why don't you tell me what it was and we can take it from there."

His wife's calm manner began to have a similar effect on John. He took a few moments to collect his thoughts, then he concentrated his attention on her once more.

"I think I; no, I did have a sort of vision last night, after I fell asleep."

Maggie frowned. "What sort of vision?"

"I saw; it was; oh bloody hell; an angel appeared in the room, if you must know."

Maggie was well beyond laughing at what she was hearing. The expression on her husband's face told her that he was experiencing some very powerful emotions, and there was certainly no humour amongst them.

She took a deep, slow breath. "All right, so you saw an angel in our bedroom last night. Was it a male or a female?"

"A male," said John.

"With wings, and a long, white robe?" Maggie continued.

John frowned as he struggled to remember. "I suppose you could call his robe white; but it was much whiter than white; like milk, but far more intense. It's very hard to describe."

"Did he speak to you?"

The strange look Maggie had seen earlier returned to John's brown eyes, and his voice was almost a whisper when he answered. "He had a message for me from; from - "

"God; was the message from God?" Maggie prompted.

John nodded.

"I see," said Maggie. "I suppose the next question is pretty obvious. What was the message, dear?"

"Recassunatem, love," said John almost casually. "God has granted us Recassunatem, or at least he will if we are willing to accept it"

Maggie frowned. "I've never heard of Recassunatem. What does it mean?"

"We are to be given a second chance; if we want it," John replied.

"But a second chance for what?" Maggie demanded impatiently. "You're not explaining properly. What does Recassunatem mean?"

"It means to be young again. Or at least for you to be twenty years old, and me to be twenty-five, and that's because I'm five years older than you already. That's what Recassunatem means; love, rebirth to adulthood: none of that pregnancy and birth business; no wasted years in growing and learning."

If Maggie wasn't so worried, she would have scolded her husband again for putting her through agony at the breakfast table. But she was well aware that his father had suffered from depression, as had one of his three brothers before eventually committing suicide, despite a great deal of medical treatment. And she had a secret dread that John could turn out to be a late sufferer of the disease.

"I suppose it must worry you, dear; having this vision?" she offered sympathetically. "Especially if it seemed that real?"

"Of course it bloody worries me!" John growled. "I mean, just think about it. How will the kids react when we end up younger than they are? And what will the grandchildren do, for Christ sakes? I can just imagine what their friends will say: they'll end up as laughing-stocks."

"Surely you're not going to take it seriously?" Maggie exclaimed. "It was just an hallucination, John! You said yourself you were asleep when it woke you up. You were probably still asleep, but sitting up; like sleepwalking, except in your case you were seeing things. Now, my guess is your mind is finding an outlet for something that's troubling you, and if that is the case you should see someone about it; a specialist perhaps. Don't those counsellors interpret these sort of things when they start having a bad effect on people. They are trained to listen to what the mind is really trying to say. Or if you don't want to go to one of them, maybe you should make an appointment with Dr Barclay. I'm sure he has come across this sort of thing many times before. You never know, you could be suffering from stress. He might even have tablets you could take to settle your mind: but if he doesn't, then you might have to think about seeing a - "

"Will you please stop going on about doctors and counsellors!" John interrupted angrily. "I knew you wouldn't believe me. I should have kept my mouth shut for the rest of the week and made the decision for both of us. After all, I'm the one who's been contacted, not you, so, by rights, the decision should be mine."

Maggie's eyes narrowed with suspicion. "What are you talking about, John; what decision? Whatever that vision was about, it's gone now; surely that's the end of it?"

Her husband became calm once more. "The angel is going to return next Sunday for an answer. There won't be another offer after that."

"I see," said Maggie. "And if we do accept; what then, John? Do we wake up next morning in our bed, as if we were back in nineteen sixty-five, and no doubt frighten our children to death when we pay them a visit? Or perhaps we will reverse slowly; say two days for each day of the week, or three days, or four? Or will it be a month for each day, or a year: that would certainly get the neighbours going. And they would probably never stop pestering us for the name of our plastic surgeon and then we would have to move, until our new neighbours found out our true age and we would be off again. Life certainly could get very complicated, you know."

"I'm being serious, Maggie!" John shouted. "But, God help me, I don't know what to do about it."

"Say yes, of course!" Maggie shot back with a false laugh. "It certainly beats the anti-ageing cream I'm using at the moment, and it's free as well."

"No it's not," John replied. "If you must know, we have to die first."

Shock stunned Maggie and her hand went to her mouth.

"I'm sorry to blurt it out like that," John carried on, guilt softening the tone of his voice, "but you had to know sooner or later."

For a few moments longer Maggie continued to stare at her husband, unable to speak. Then a fierce determination drove the shock away. "Now listen to me, John," she said in a strong tone, "this nonsense has gone far enough. I knew when I came down that something must be troubling you. And I listened as you told me about your experience during the night. But when you start talking about dying, then it's time to pull yourself together. Now, it's clear to me that there is something on your mind. Maybe your retirement is having a negative effect on your confidence. That could be why you saw an angel in the room, offering to change your life to, oh, I don't know; to send you back to a working age. You were obviously far happier then than you are now."

"That's rubbish!" John snapped. "I'm perfectly happy with my retirement. In fact I was looking forward to it for years. How do you think we can afford a house like this, and a kitchen any professional cook would give his right arm for; because I prepared for my retirement, of course. And yes, I did love that job. But I didn't want to do it forever. The last few years were physically as well as mentally taxing. And I was glad when it was time for me to retire, especially since I was ready for it. When my colleagues were out drinking, or gambling, or buying flash cars, or spending money like it would never stop coming, I was saving every penny because I knew that if I wanted the both of us to enjoy my retirement and not just exist through it, I would need money. And I can tell you this, not for a single second of the six months I've been retired have I had even the smallest regret. I'm happy, Maggie; that's right; I'm living my life just as I always wanted to live it. So don't go telling me that I'm hallucinating about a previous existence; that I know damn well I wanted out of. And if anyone has regrets about retirement, it's going to be you. I was asked to stay on at that advertising agency, in fact they begged me, but I turned down the offer. Whereas you had to retire once you reached sixty. Everyone had to in that antiquated stock broking firm. So look in the mirror if you want to see who is having trouble with their retirement. If anyone is having difficulty about giving up work, it will be you."

"I'm not the one having visions, John," Maggie countered, "you are. Anyway, you're quite wrong about me. I admit I was sad to leave my job, after all, I worked in that firm for twenty-seven years and I enjoyed it. But I was also looking forward to both of us being at home together, doing all the things we talked about without being restricted by work. So you needn't worry about me; I have the life I want; or at least I did have until now."

John ran his fingers through his hair and began to shake his head.

Regret and pity welled up inside Maggie, and she rushed to his side. She put her arms around him, hugging him tight.

"I'm so sorry, dear, I didn't mean to be confrontational. It's just that you're frightening me. Normally you would have laughed about this dream of yours, and - "

"It wasn't a dream, love," John interrupted, his voice urgent. "I swear it wasn't. I could tell. When I woke up this morning, it felt as real as every other thing that happened yesterday. Why won't you believe me? You said yourself that normally I would laugh it off. Surely the fact that I haven't must prove to you that it was more than a dream?"

Maggie hugged her husband even tighter and kissed the top of his head. "Of course I believe it was more than just a dream. But I don't believe it's as clear-cut as you think. You must be very worried about something, and this angel is your subconscious letting you know so that you can do something about it. As for God sending you an angel with an offer of a second chance to live your life over again, well, that's just not done, now is it, dear? God doesn't do that. We only get one chance at life. I don't think he would even consider changing a rule that has probably existed as long as life has been on the planet."

John raised his face and looked into his wife's eyes. "I don't care what you think, love, it wasn't a product of my mind," he said in a calm tone. "The angel was real; I know he was."

Maggie placed a quick kiss on his forehead. "Then if that's what you want to believe, dear, you go right ahead and believe it. After all, thousands of people claim to have seen angels; even felt their presence. So whom am I to cast doubt on their existence: but promise me one thing, will you, let's have no more talk of dying. You know death has always held a horror for me, ever since I watched my grandmother die of that terrible disease."

Colour returned to John's pale features. "All I can promise is not to discuss it any more today, if you promise not to try and convince me I was dreaming?"

Maggie ruffled his hair and smiled. "You got yourself a deal there, pardner. Now, how about some breakfast: I'm sure we're both starving."

CHAPTER THREE

Tuesday 8th June

Maggie settled on the telephone seat in the hall, and lifted the receiver to her ear. Her left hand hovered over the push buttons for a moment. She was undecided about taking her problems beyond the confines of their home, but no matter how hard she tried she could not prevent thoughts of John's family history of depression leaping in and out of her mind.

Then she pressed the numbers.

"Hello?" said a female voice almost immediately.

"Hello, Jennifer dear," said Maggie. "It's me; mum."

"Hi, mum! What's up?"

"Oh, nothing much, dear. Just wondering if you'd like to pop round for a coffee; if you're not too busy, that is?"

"Well, I am in the middle of something at the moment," said Jennifer. "It's ten-thirty now, but I should be finished by four; that do?"

"Oh, don't worry about it," Maggie said hurriedly. "Another time will be fine."

"Are you all right, mum?" came the reply. "You sound a bit strange?"

Maggie laughed, but it came out false and a little desperate. "Of course I'm all right, dear. Can't a mother give her daughter a call without something being wrong."

"Now I know something is wrong!" Jennifer declared. "I'll be round soon. Where's dad?"

"He's at the golf club. He won't be back until five."

"You two haven't had a fight, have you?" said Jennifer accusingly.

"Your father and I; goodness no! We never fight, dear. We just talk loudly to one another at times."

"Right; that's it," said Jennifer. "You're really worrying me now, mum. See you in fifty, and no arguments."

Maggie put the receiver down slowly, wondering if she was doing the right thing involving her daughter. Of her three children, Jennifer was the most level-headed, and her job was to help people with their problems. But psychology was hardly her expertise. Would she have even the slightest idea what to do about her father?

Maggie jumped when the door bell rang.

She was shocked to discover that she had not moved from the seat, and that it was her daughter at the door. Only Jennifer did that five staccato rings of the bell.

She opened the door with a trembling hand and Jennifer came through with a frown of annoyance on her face.

"Bloody traffic!" she cried. "Sorry I'm a bit later than I said, mum, but I got stuck behind some idiot. Why lorry drivers have to hog the whole road, I don't know. I didn't get past him until we got to the roundabout, and then he had the nerve to flash his lights at me; bloody cheek. I should have taken his number and complained to the police."

"That's all right, dear," said Maggie with a weak smile. "You go on through to the living-room, and I'll make us some coffee."

Jennifer Barclay was a beautiful young woman. She was five feet nine inches tall, with the slim and sexy figure that was often seen on the catwalks of the world. She had large, intense green eyes; high cheekbones; generous lips that never needed the touch of lipstick, and the most stunning long, red hair that turned men's heads in the street. Many people would have bet their life savings that Jennifer Barclay would end up in fashion someday. But then they didn't understand that her mind was just as beautiful as her body. She had an excellent grasp of mathematics, politics, the arts, and almost every aspect of the legal system and its complex workings. She would succeed at whatever she set her mind to, because she was ambitious as well as brilliant. And despite her father's misgivings about the workload she carried, she knew that one day she would make him proud of her success in her chosen profession.

"Here we are, dear," said Maggie as she eventually came into the living-room with two china cups of coffee on a solid silver tray she kept for special occasions.

Jennifer laughed. "For Heaven sakes, mum, don't treat me like a guest. You know very well any old cracked mug will do me. I suppose the cucumber sandwiches are coming next."

Maggie placed the tray on the coffee table and sat next to her on the settee. "Can't I spoil my favourite daughter once in a while."

"Course you can, mum," said Jennifer, leaning over and kissing her mother on the cheek.

Maggie suddenly burst out crying and covered her face with her hands.

Startled, Jennifer put her arms around her. "Oh my God: mum; what's the matter? You're not sick are you?"

Maggie shook her head, but continued crying.

Jennifer's shock turned to confusion. "It's not dad, is it? Please, mum, tell me what's wrong?"

Maggie took her hands from her face and straightened her shoulders. She pulled a tissue from her sleeve and wiped her eyes. "Don't mind me, dear. I'm just being silly. Both your father and I are in perfect health."

Jennifer looked puzzled. "Then what's the matter? I've never seen you so upset."

Maggie stared at her daughter. "It's your father, Jennifer. I'm terribly worried about him."

"You just said that he was in perfect health?" Jennifer protested. "And since dad would no more look at another woman than take up ballet classes, what on Earth can he have done to upset you like this?"

Maggie laughed, genuinely this time. "I'm sure you're going to tell me that I'm creating a great big fuss about nothing, but, you see, dear, your father has had a dream; or rather, as he insists, a vision."

Jennifer frowned. "A vision: what sort of vision?"

"It was an angel, dear," said Maggie.

Jennifer's eyes were wide with surprise. "Good grief! You mean he saw a glowing, celestial figure; what; dressed in white: floating in the sky: that sort of thing?"

"Yes, dear, but it was in the bedroom, and as far as I know he wasn't glowing. However, it seems he did have wings, and he was dressed in white."

"I was joking, mum!" Jennifer exclaimed incredulously.

"I'm afraid it's not a joking matter," said Maggie, gravely. "It should be, of course; but it isn't. Your father believes an angel appeared to him and nothing will convince him it was a dream, despite the fact that it was: I mean it had to be."

"Of course it was, mum," said Jennifer, looking nonplussed. "After all, Hampstead is hardly Lourdes, now is it. And any water suddenly gushing up in one of its streets would only have the water company arriving with diggers and those horrible cones, and where would the religious symbolism be in that."

The humour was clearly lost on her mother as her expression remained serious.

Jennifer cleared her throat in embarrassment. "Sorry, mum, didn't mean to be flippant about something that is clearly upsetting you very much. Now, let's get the facts clear: so dad believes he met an angel, and obviously he doesn't think it was all just a dream or you wouldn't be in the state you are. Was it a famous angel or just an ordinary one; assuming there is such a thing as an angel that is ordinary?"

"You're still not taking this seriously," her mother scolded, wiping her nose with a tissue.

"Yes I am, mum," Jennifer protested. "I'm just trying to get my head around it. Now, what was an angel doing in your bedroom?"

Maggie stared at her daughter. "I know you'll find this hard to believe, dear, but your father thinks God sent the angel to give him a very special message."

Jennifer started to laugh, but managed to suppress it. A joke popped into her head also, but she managed to suppress that too.

"I quite understand why you would think it's funny," said Maggie, "but, I promise you, it isn't. You should have seen your father this morning. I found him sitting at the kitchen table as if he had the troubles of the whole world on his shoulders. He was so intense; so distraught by his experience that I thought he might be losing his mind."

"Retirement!" Jennifer exclaimed with a loudness that always made her colleagues at work jump. "Of course; how silly of me not to see it straight away: that will be what's behind this so-called vision of his. I knew he was too young to retire at sixty-five. He has the mind and body of a forty year old. He should be back at work, practically running that Advertising Firm as he used to; not pottering around in the garden, and sitting in front of the TV all day."

" I suggested that to him," said Maggie, "and he nearly bit my head off. He told me, quite firmly too, that he is enjoying every minute of his retirement and he even suggested that if anyone was missing work, it was me."

"You're not; are you?" Jennifer asked.

"I'm perfectly happy with my life the way it is," said Maggie, firmly, "and I don't want it to change in any way. That's why this business with your father is worrying me so much."

Jennifer began tapping her lower teeth with the thumbnail of her right hand, as she always did when faced with a perplexing mystery. "This doesn't sound like dad, one little bit. Perhaps there's a clue in the message from the angel. What exactly did he tell him, and don't leave out anything at all? The answer to all this could be in the smallest detail."

"Well, " Maggie seemed unsure about answering, as if the message from the angel, rather than the appearance of the angel himself, might alter her daughter's perception of what was going on, "it seems that God has offered John, and me, a second chance to live our lives over again. John said it was something called Recassunatem."

"Interesting." Jennifer was intrigued, and stared fixedly at her mother as if she was a new client with a fascinating problem. "Go on, mum; tell me more."

"Oh, this is preposterous!" Maggie cried suddenly slapping her knees with her hands. "I don't know what I was thinking; dragging you all the way over here because your father had a silly dream."

"Don't stop now, mum!" Jennifer exploded, her hands becoming fists in anticipation. "I want to know the rest of it. How do you mean a second chance, and I'm not moving until you tell me, and you know how stubborn your daughter can be!"

Maggie laughed despite herself. "Very well, dear. I must confess, it will be a relief to get it off my chest. So, here goes. Your father and I are to have our youth back. I am going to be twenty years old, and your father twenty-five, because, as you know, he is five years older than me. Now, what do you think of that?"

Jennifer returned to tapping her teeth. "A desire to be young again: turning back the clock," she said thoughtfully. "Hmmm, I suppose dad could be suffering a strange form of mid-life crisis, and whereas other men start colouring their hair; buying sports cars, and chasing after dolly birds, my dad starts getting visits from angels: trust him to be different."

Jennifer then reached out and took her mother's hands in hers. She smiled warmly. "Listen to me, mum, I don't think for a single second that you have anything to worry about. Dad will come to his senses eventually. If he was planning to change his life in some way, he wouldn't bother with visions: he'd be doing something: taking action. You know what he's like: the direct approach has always been his motto. He sees a problem and goes right to the heart of it. Why do you think they called him 'The Tick Tock Man' in that Agency; because they had deadlines, and dad made damn sure his work was completed in time. He never once exceeded a deadline, even if it meant staying on through the night. So, try not to worry, dad will take stock of this peculiar situation and find a way to solve it. All you have to do is give him a little time."

"But he only has until Sunday, dear," Maggie protested.

Jennifer pulled a face in astonishment. "You mean there's some kind of time limit on this offer: is God that busy?"

"Don't mock, dear," said Maggie. "The angel is going to return in the early hours of Sunday morning, and your father must have an answer for him."

"So, when did he have this vision?" Jennifer asked.

"Sunday," Maggie replied.

"You didn't say anything about this when we came round for dinner yesterday?" Jennifer protested.

Maggie hesitated. "I thought it best not to bring the subject up when you and your father were in the same room, dear. You can be rather, well, over-determined to tackle a problem head on, if you know what I mean. And since your father was still in an difficult mood, I didn't want to risk a serious argument developing between the two of you."

"I suppose not," Jennifer agreed with some reluctance. "Still, an opportunity missed, and all that."

A frown appeared on Maggie's face. "There is something else I haven't told you, dear. You see, we both have to die first before we can become young again."

"Hmmm; reincarnation; that makes sense." Jennifer pursed her lips and stared across the room for a few moments. Then she looked at her mother again. "Right, mum, this is what you do. Tell dad to tell the angel you accept the offer. After all, what harm can it do. As far as dad's concerned, the angel comes back next Sunday: dad tells him that you both wish to be young again: the angel takes your decision back to God, and Bob's-Your-Uncle, problem solved. You both carry on as you have always done; enjoying your lives and being the most wonderful parents in the whole world, I might add. Then you both return as a young couple after you have passed on, which won't be for a very long time because you are bound to live into your nineties, the both of you being so young-looking and healthy. Who knows, maybe there is something in this reincarnation business. Maybe we all return as young adults, and it's just that you and dad have been told about it while you're still alive; you lucky dogs!"

"I don't know," Maggie replied slowly, and not totally convinced. "You make it all sound so simple and easy."

"Life is only as complicated and hard as you make it," said Jennifer authoritatively. "Or as my boss always says in that deep voice of his when he's telling someone off for spending too much time on one task 'Why count the holes in a crumpet before deciding how much butter to put on it.' I have to try very hard not to laugh when he says it to me, because he doesn't have any sense of humour. Anyway, mum, everything will work out if you give it time."

Maggie's face lit up. "You think so, dear? You really think that's all I have to do, and this terrible business will be over?"

"Sure of it, mum," Jennifer declared. Then she stood up. "My bill will be dropping through your letterbox in a few days, with one hell of a thump, but make dad pay it. Now, I better be going. I have a pile of paperwork sitting next to the iron, and I'm back at work on Wednesday."

"We haven't had our coffee?" said Maggie, standing also.

Jennifer gave her mother a peck on the cheek. "Next time, mum. I'll see myself out, and don't worry too much."

CHAPTER FOUR

Wednesday 9th June

John reached across the breakfast table for a bottle of brown sauce.

Maggie tutted as he then proceeded to drizzle the thick, brown liquid over everything on his plate.

"Not too much of that, dear," she scolded, "you'll smother the taste of your breakfast."

John grinned and continued drizzling. "Surely you must know that this particular sauce is the perfect accompaniment to sausages, bacon, eggs and mushrooms, love. And it must be true because it says so on the bottle."

Maggie grinned back. "I'll bet Gary Rhodes doesn't smother his food like that, and he's famous for promoting English cuisine."

John put the sauce bottle down and pointed his fork, with an end of sausage still on it, at his wife. "That is an outrageous assumption, love. Gary Rhodes probably isn't allowed to advertise commercial sauces on his programmes. You mark my words; though; have a look in his cupboards at home and I'll bet you'll find at least half a dozen different kinds of the stuff. He may be a famous chef, but he's still just a man, British and proud of it when he's in his castle."

"Then we must put this discussion on hold until he invites us on a tour of his kitchen," said Maggie with a twinkle in her eyes. "But for heavens sake, dear, don't invite him here. I don't want the two of you having a kitchen war. He's got more money than we have, and you are a poor loser."

A startled expression appeared on John's face. "Me; lose; in a war of the kitchens: never! I'd make that stickyup hair of his wilt with envy should he ever be lucky enough to tour my pride-and-joy."

"Thinking about it, you're probably right, dear," Maggie conceded. "Anyway, I saw him on TV the other day and his hair doesn't stick up any more. He looks quite normal, now."

John laughed. "I stand corrected, but it still goes about my kitchen., and I'm glad to see you in a joking mood, love. After Sunday I thought you might start fretting about what happened."

"We can't let these things get us down," Maggie replied. "All I want is for our lives to return to normal."

It was as if Maggie had reached out and given her husband a very hard slap across the face.

His eyes were wide and staring, and his knife and fork banged on the plate when he put them down.

"What do you mean, Maggie?" he demanded. "How can we return to normal? We only have until Saturday to decide if we're going to accept the offer?"

Maggie struggled to keep calm. "Of course we must accept, dear. After all, it isn't every day that something like this comes along."

John's expression softened. "Then you've already decided. I'm so glad, love. I was worried that you wouldn't make up your mind in time."

"I see no point in over-discussing the matter," Maggie replied. "In some ways my answer was a forgone conclusion. You know I have a great fear of death, and when my time comes; hopefully not for twenty years or so, it will be comforting to know that I will be reincarnated into my young body. Oh, I know I was never beautiful, but I was never short of male attention before you came along."

John stared silently at his wife. The new expression on his face was unreadable.

"What's the matter, dear?" she asked. "Have I said something wrong?"

"You said reincarnated?" John replied in a low voice. "Why did you say reincarnated?"

"Because that is what it is, isn't it: you come to the end of one life, and then you begin another. And with us, we come back to our own bodies, only a lot younger."

"No, no, no!" John retorted, his eyes bulging in frustration. "That's not how it's going to be at all. Haven't you been listening? You don't carry on with your old life until it runs out. You have to trade in your old life for the new one: I thought you understood that?"

"I do now," said Maggie, hiding her alarm at her husband's outburst, "only because you have just explained it to me. So, how does this thing work? How do we trade our lives?"

"I thought that was obvious," John sighed. "You just give up the old one. Look, Maggie, I don't understand why you are behaving like this. You tell me you accept, then you carry on as if you want to avoid the gift God is offering you. All I want to do is improve our lives: why do you have to put obstacles in my way?"

A touch of anger tightened Maggie's lips. "I didn't realize I was," she said coldly.

"Well you are!" John shot back. "Now, it's simple. I'll tell the angel that we are ready to give up our lives, and before we know it, we will be young again. But we have to die first: is that clear enough now?"

The Colour of the Young

"Yes, John," Maggie replied. "So how long will it be before that happens; dying, I mean?"

John shrugged. "I'm not sure; a few months probably. It all depends on what disease we get."

Maggie's heart almost stopped. "Disease?" she whispered.

"The disease that kills us, of course," said John. "Surely you didn't think we would drift off to sleep one night and wake up younger the following morning, did you?"

"You mean we are going to get some terrible illness that will slowly kill us?" said Maggie.

John nodded. Then suddenly he reached across the table and took his wife's hands in his. His manner became pleading but at the same time excited. "Oh, I know this sort of thing frightens you, love; but I promise; just a short period of discomfort and we will have another fifty years together; perhaps more. Just think what we can do with that time. We can go dancing again; clubbing I think they call it these days, and the holidays we can have."

"We can do all those things now, dear," Maggie answered trying to stop her voice from trembling. "After all, neither of us are infirm, and we can certainly afford a couple of holidays a year?"

John pulled back, his mood turning sour. "It wouldn't be the same. I'm sixty-five years old. I want to be young again. I want to have the energy to live life to the full. If you must know, Maggie, I'm sick to death of watching this blasted, creeping grey hair gradually replacing my natural black colour, and these lines on my face; I swear they are doubling every six months. So, if you want to know whether I'm willing to put up with a little bit of pain in order to reverse all that, then you can bet this house I am."

"I didn't realize you felt that way about getting old," said Maggie. "You never said anything."

John shrugged. "What would have been the point. You couldn't have done anything about it. That's the thing about ageing, isn't it: the inevitable decaying of your body and not being able to do a damn thing to stop it, or even slow it down. You know, when one of my plants in the garden gets like that, I pull it out and throw it on the compost heap where it belongs."

"What about my lines and grey hairs, John?" said Maggie, a haunted expression on her face. "Have you been watching them as intently as you obviously have your own?"

John's eyes lowered in embarrassment before Maggie's accusing stare. "Of course not, love. You are just as attractive to me now as you were forty years ago. I'm only talking about myself."

"Are you, John? Well, it seems to me that anyone obsessed with the normal signs that go with ageing will have no choice but to apply those concerns to anyone close to them. And tell me something else, John, if you did wake up in the morning only twenty-five years old, would you see me as attractive as you said I was, or just an old woman, and don't bother trying to deny that my age wouldn't be a problem: it's only natural that you would find me far too old for you?"

"You're not being fair, love," said John, clearly disturbed by his wife's questions.

"I may not be fair, dear, but I am being truthful. If that distresses you, then I can only say that it's your own fault. After all, you started this."

Maggie then left the kitchen and made her way to the living-room. Her husband had shocked her to her very soul, and she felt a terrible dread that the man she had invested her whole life in, might turn out, after all these years, to be a stranger.

She sat on the settee and John dropped down next to her a few moments later.

He wanted desperately to comfort his wife, but he could not find words that wouldn't sound insincere. She would be expecting him to apologise and try and make things right, but once said, certain admissions could never be retracted; the truth more so than any other.

CHAPTER FIVE

Thursday 10th June

Jennifer put the file she had in her right hand on the table and picked up the telephone receiver.

"Hi, lucky you, I'm in for a change?"

"Jennifer; it's mum."

Jennifer's heart lurched. Every hour of the day since her last talk with her mother she was expecting bad news, and perhaps this was it. "What's the matter, mum? Has something else happened?"

"It's your father, dear!" Maggie sobbed. "He's worse. Now he's talking about the two of us getting some horrible illness that will kill us."

"Right, enough is enough!" Jennifer snapped. "Having a dream about being young again is one thing, but I won't have dad upsetting you like this. I'm coming round and have it out with him. Is he in?"

"He's in the garden, dear. I'd rather come and see you, if you don't mind. Your father is in too much of a mood for a confrontation and I don't want you two having a serious falling out. I just couldn't bear that."

A loud sigh shot from Jennifer. "Oh, all right, mum, of course you can call round. I've finished the work I needed to do. I can drop it into the firm in the morning."

"Thanks, dear," said Maggie. "I'll be there in an hour."

"Bye, mom."

"Bye, dear."

Jennifer put the receiver down and picked up the file. She crossed the living-room floor to an oak sideboard and put the file in a drawer. Then she made her way to the pale blue settee and dropped into it. Despite her earlier conviction about her father, in truth she was worried about him. There was a history of depression on his side of the family, and she knew what this debilitating illness could do. One of her colleagues, Sarah Jenkins, had suffered for years with it, until it finally became too much for her. The last she heard of Sarah she was hospitalised somewhere in Cornwall, and the thought of her youthful father ending up the same way, was unbearable.

A number of times she considered phoning her brothers, but decided to wait until her mother arrived. If the problem could be sorted out quickly and quietly, there would be no point in causing unnecessary worry for the rest of the family.

When Maggie arrived, red-eyed and drawn-looking, Jennifer put her arm around her and guided her to the settee. She was shocked at how distraught her mother was, and mentally scolded her father.

"Right then, mum," she declared with a firmness she did not feel, "what has dad been doing now to put you in such a state, again?"

Half an hour later Maggie finished telling her daughter the whole story. Jennifer didn't interrupted once, preferring not to impede the desperate outpourings from her mother, in case some vital point was missed.

"What are we going to do, dear?" Maggie added. "I know you told me to humour him, but that was before he began talking about dying within the next few months from some disease?"

"You're both in good health, aren't you?" Jennifer replied. "So, when neither of you gets sick, surely dad will realize that he was wrong about the angel?"

"Oh no, not your father," said Maggie firmly. "Don't you see, he will treat this like one of those problems he used to deal with at work."

"What do you mean?" said Jennifer. "When the disease fails to materialise, he'll have no choice but to accept that he was wrong."

Maggie's fear was rising again. "You still don't understand, Jennifer," she said. "I know your father. When we remain healthy, instead of rejecting the vision, he'll reject his interpretation of it. Remember what he always used to say. Whenever you find yourself with a problem that seems to be insurmountable; always look in the mirror, because the cause of the problem's invincibility may be looking right back at you."

Jennifer stared uncomprehending at her mother. Then her eyes reflected the horror of her sudden understanding, and a gasp left her lips.

"Precisely," said Maggie. "Your father may come to believe that we must take our own lives."

"Oh my God!" Jennifer cried. "Surely you don't think he'll take it that far?"

"I don't know what to think. This obsession is controlling him; I'm sure of that. A week ago I would have laughed at any suggestion that your father would ever behave like he's behaving now. But look at me; I'm not laughing, am I: no, I'm sitting in my daughter's living-room, discussing my husband's sanity, and whether he plans to kill us both in a few months time because an angel has told him to."

"Oh, mum," said Jennifer, tears filling her eyes, "please try not to worry too much. If dad is planning to do something crazy, he's not going to do it yet. I'll talk to Robert and Mark. I'm sure we'll come up with a solution to this problem before you know it."

"What can you possibly do, dear?" Maggie replied. "Your father has always known his own mind, and come to think of it, I don't believe he has ever asked me for advice about anything. Oh, he often agrees with my decisions, but he always sticks by his own. I know you will say that's because he's a stubborn man; but he isn't really: it's just that in his job he was the one who had to come up with the solutions to problems. His colleagues accepted that and so have I. Anyway, if truth be told, his way usually turned out to be the best way. So you see, dear, no one in the family has ever had the need to go against him before. I have no idea at all how he will react if we start now."

"Then it's time we found out," Jennifer replied firmly, wiping her eyes. "I am not going to allow dad to wreck your marriage, because that's what he is doing, mum. Oh, he may not realize he is, but that's no excuse. You both mean so much to us and there is no way we are going to stand by and do nothing."

"I suppose you're right," Maggie conceded.

"Course I am," said Jennifer. "Now, you sit there and I'll get us a drink; something a little stronger than tea, I think."

CHAPTER SIX

Thursday 10th June

Mark Pemberton roared with laughter and began coughing as some of the food in his mouth slipped down his throat the wrong way. "Christ, Jen," he exclaimed through coughs, "are you trying to kill me: dad; getting visits from an angel: you have got to be kidding!"

"I'm being serious!" Jennifer snapped, pale with anger.

Mark's whole body shook as he tried to control the laughter. "I thought mum was his angel; he said it often enough. Mind you, that must have been quite a shock for her. Imagine opening her eyes to see dad's fantasy standing in her bedroom."

"For your information this angel was a male," Jennifer replied.

Mark's mouth dropped open in mock surprise. "I never knew dad could bat for the other side. He's sure turning out to be quite a character in his dotage, isn't he."

"Do you know something, Mark," Jennifer hissed, "I've had clients even more difficult than Rupert Murdoch, but not one of them could wind me up like you do! I don't know why I bothered telling you. You can't be serious about anything."

Mark reached out and grabbed his sister's arm as she stood up to leave. The laughter stopped, and his expression became serious.

"Sit down, Jen, for Christ sakes! How did you expect me to react? You invite me and Rob for lunch because something serious has come up. And then you tell us that dad has had a visit from an angel. Did you expect me to clasp my hands together; give you a thoughtful look and say, how interesting, Jen, and was it Gabriel, by any chance?"

Jennifer looked around the restaurant. Many of the lunch-time diners were looking back, but quickly returned their attention to their meal.

Embarrassed, she sat down slowly, and took a sip of her coffee.

Mark and Robert, who were sitting opposite her, waited for her to speak.

"He might be sick, you know," she whispered forcefully to Mark after a while. "Did you think of that?"

"Rubbish," Mark grunted. "Dad's not the type to get brain problems. I spent most of last Tuesday with him; remember? If there was anything wrong with him I'd have seen it. And another thing, I don't know very much about depression, but I don't believe for one minute that you just wake up one morning with it. Am I right, Rob?"

Robert Pemberton shrugged. "Couldn't say, Mark. I don't know about these things either, but if Jen and mum are worried, then the matter should be taken seriously."

Mark glared at his brother. "Always the diplomat, Rob," he declared. "Now, if it was anything to do with your business, you'd be all claws and teeth making your opinion felt."

"That's because if it concerned my business, I'd know what I was talking about," Robert replied testily. "Anyway, I'm not impulsive like you, but that's probably why I don't make so many mistakes as you do."

"I didn't invite the both of you here to start arguing amongst yourselves," Jennifer scolded.

"Who's arguing," said Mark. "Rob is sitting on the fence, and I'm, well, I'm just being a total prat as usual."

Jennifer smiled at her brother. How like his father he was in certain ways; six feet three inches tall, with the same thin frame; rugged, handsome face, and jet black hair. But his temperament was quite different. Where her father was a level-headed man with a determined streak and a sense of humour that had a certain dryness to it, Mark was impetuous; outrageously funny at times, unreliable, and without a single shred of ambition, yet absolutely adorable. Jennifer could never decide which of the tall men in her life was her favourite.

Robert Pemberton was different than both his father and his brother. He was three years older than Mark, and one year younger than his sister. He took after his mother's side of the family, with the same dark brown hair, now receding, and the same round face which was a little on the plump side. He was just five feet seven inches tall, and had a powerful, stocky build that was running to fat in recent years. He had the same gentle temperament as his mother, but hated westerns.

Jennifer loved Robert in a different way to Mark, but certainly just as much.

"So what are we going to do about dad?" Mark continued. "Do you think we could get him to see a doctor?"

"Out of the question," said Robert. "If you even hint at medical help to dad, he'll take that as a sign that we don't believe in his vision."

"We don't!" Mark exclaimed, spreading his hands across the table and knocking over a salt seller. He hurriedly picked it up.

"Of course we don't," Robert replied, "but we can't tell dad that. It would probably drive a wedge between us, and he would never agree to anything we suggested. No, with dad you have to take it slow. He's no fool. He'll have worked out that mum has told us, and so he'll be watching for any sighs of negativity."

"So it's a white van in the early hours: a tap on the head, and the nut house," Mark declared.

Robert scowled at his brother. "Can't you be serious about anything."

"I'm trying very hard not to," Mark answered, taking another bite of the sandwich on his plate.

"I wish you two would stop this bickering," Jennifer pleaded. "Mum's worried sick. We have to do something."

"Look, Jen," said Mark, "there is nothing we can do without talking to dad. He's not a child, and we have no control over what he thinks and does. All we can do is have a word with him. Why don't one of us take him out for a drink and talk things over. And when we make him see the effect he's having on mum, he's bound to come to his senses. Dad has never been the cruel type. He'd do anything for mum; even give up getting visits from angels, if he knew she was suffering."

"That's an excellent idea," Robert said cheerfully, "and since you came up with it, you can carry it out. Go easy on him, though, he may be in a more fragile state than you're used to."

Mark's hands went up defensively. "Hey, wait a minute! This is deep, family stuff, and completely out of my league. Both of you are far more qualified to handle this situation."

"Dad will listen to you," Jennifer countered. "Although he would never admit this to mum, he admires your wild streak, and the way you never get yourself bogged down. That could be what this is all about; dad looking for the freedom you have."

"You're wrong there," Mark protested. "Don't you know your physics: two negatives always repel each other. It's opposites that attract."

"This is family, not science," said Robert, "and we still live in a democratic country, don't we?"

Mark looked puzzled. "So?"

"So, all those in favour of Mark speaking to dad?" Robert declared, and his hand shot up, but Jennifer's beat him to it.

"Democracy wins again," Robert grinned. "Now I must be getting back before that idiot Simon pay's out two thousand pounds for a fake Ming bowl like he did last week."

"I have to go too, I'm afraid," said Jennifer. "Peter is coming home early today so we can take the kids to the park. And, go easy on dad, Mark. You know how important this is to mum."

"Hey; wait a minute!" Mark cried as his brother and sister quickly made their way out of the restaurant. "I didn't get a chance to vote. What kind of democracy is that?"

Sniggers from two young girls sitting at another table drew Mark's attention. He smiled sheepishly at them. "See what happens when you're the brains of the family."

CHAPTER SEVEN

Friday 11th June

The rain was pouring from the sky like some biblical act of judgement as Mark dashed from his parked car to the pub entrance. Like many people in Hampstead that night, he had been caught out by the unexpected rain, and regretted not bringing a coat.

"What the devil happened to global warming," he grumbled as he entered The Marathon.

The place was packed and Mark had to push his way to the bar.

He had a quick look around and spotted his father at the other end of the bar, drinking what looked like whisky. His father was strictly a real ale drinker, and Mark was puzzled by the change.

They hadn't even spoken yet and already he saw a cause for concern. He hoped it wasn't a sign of things to come.

John saw his son and waved.

Mark waved back, and made his way through the throng to his father's side.

"Usual, son?" said John, smiling.

Mark nodded.

"Lager and another one of these, please," John requested when he caught the attention of one of the three bartenders.

"Trying something different, dad?" Mark asked as casually as he could.

John held up his glass and stared at the golden liquid inside. "I used to be a whisky drinker when I was your age, but I decided to give it up."

"Too expensive?" said Mark.

John smiled. "Too nice. I was drinking it like beer, so I decided that since the whisky had no intention of giving me up, I had to give it up. It was hard at first. Beer is such a different drink, and took quite some getting used to. To be perfectly honest, at first it tasted like watered-down disinfectant, but I persevered, and I also decided to make a study of the beers sold locally; you know; treat it like one of my advertising projects. Anyway, I eventually got to like the stuff; especially the hoppie-tasting brands."

The ordered drink's arrived.

John finished his glass, then handed Mark his lager.

"Cheers, dad," said Mark.

John picked up the second glass. "Cheers, son."

"So," said Mark, wiping foam from his top lip, "you've decided to go back on the whisky: any particular reason?"

John shrugged. "No. Just thought I'd see if it tasted the same as it used to?"

"Does it?"

John stared fixedly at his son. His expression grave. "Nothing tastes the same as it did when you were young, Mark. Your taste buds get dulled by time. You think they don't bake bread properly anymore because of the taste, but again it's the old taste buds, getting decrepit like the rest of your body."

"Steady on, dad," Mark laughed. "As a matter of fact they don't bake bread properly anymore. I'm young, and even I can tell the difference."

"Good for you, son," said John, suddenly losing interest in the conversation.

"This place has changed a bit since its makeover last year," said Mark after a while. "I remember when you

The Colour of the Young

wouldn't get more than a dozen people in here at a time: look at it now."

"Is that why you invited me here, Mark; to see what's been done to my old watering hole?" said John.

"Course not," said Mark, suddenly bothered by the close proximity of other people. "I just thought we could have a bit of a chat."

John frowned. "About what?"

"Well; about; about anything you like, I suppose."

"Would angels be a suitable topic?" said John with a hint of irritation in his tone.

"Oh, look, dad," said Mark hurriedly, "I don't want to discuss this any more than you probably do, but I've been picked to do the dirty work, so let's get it over with, shall we."

John's eyebrows arched. "It's not like you to get yourself lumbered like this. How did those two fox's manage it?"

"Democratic vote," Mark replied with a sigh.

John grinned. "Oh, that one. I remember they used to get you into all sorts of mischief when you were kids, with *'The Vote.'* I'm surprised you're still falling for it."

Mark shrugged. "What can I say. Some people never learn. But, look here, dad, what's all this nonsense? Mum is frantic with worry that you might end up harming yourself."

John turned away and took a sip of his drink. His shoulders went back, a sure sign to Mark that his father was now entering an aggressive, defensive mode.

"That's between your mother and me, son. So, drop the subject, will you."

"Sorry, dad, no can do," said Mark. "I didn't want to be involved, but I am. I owe it to Mum and the others to take back an assurance that you won't do anything stupid."

John spun round suddenly, his face twisted with rage. "What the hell do you know about stupidity!" he hissed through clenched teeth. "The only time I ever see a look of worry in your mother's eyes is when we're discussing you and your so-called future. All you do is waste your life with a woman who is totally unsuitable; bouncing from job to job like some demented ping-pong ball, and totally oblivious to the fact that you're hurting your mother. So, don't talk to me about stupidity until you learn to curb your own."

"That's not fair!" Mark hissed back. "I'm entitled to live my life any way I choose, and for your information, dad, Tracy is suitable. Ok, so she may not have Jennifer's brains, or Robert's business acumen, but she's a kind, witty, loving young woman, with a generous heart and an honesty that would make the Pope blush with shame."

"Then you should respect the way I want to live my life," John countered.

"Your life is more complicated than mine," said Mark. "Any decisions that have to be made, Tracy and I make them together. And if one of us is opposed to something, then it's discarded. After all, where would be the fun in anything if one of us was resentful about it. Now mum is obviously unhappy with what you are doing, so you should stop. Or doesn't her happiness count for anything?"

Silence then reigned between the two men as they were lost in their own thoughts and emotions.

Mark was the first to give in. "Oh; come on, dad," he pleaded, "what's all this rubbish about? I thought you and mum were happy together? What's happened to change that? I mean, she's not having an affair, is she?"

John gave an exasperated sigh. "Don't be ridiculous," he said in a low voice. "Your mother would never dream of being unfaithful, and even if she was interested in someone else, she would divorce me before she even went out with him; you should know that."

"What is it then?"

"You know very well what it is, son. It's just that, like the rest of the family, you can't accept it so you're looking for a different truth. Well, there isn't one. Now, if you don't mind, I'd like you to drop the subject. Anyway, how are things; decided to settle down yet? It would make your mother very happy if you did, and isn't that the reason you're here; to put her mind at rest."

"No, dad, I'm not ready to settle down yet," said Mark. "When the time is right I will and mum will be the first to know since my plans are such a worry to her."

"Well, don't leave it too long," John offered, ignoring the dig. "Haven't you noticed; the older you get, the faster time goes. Nature is always trying to catch you out, and the trick is to keep one jump ahead."

Mark gave his father a humourless grin, and decided to drop the matter. "Thanks, dad; I'll remember to keep jumping."

CHAPTER EIGHT

Friday 11th June

Jennifer handed her brother a cup of coffee, and sat next to him on the settee. He was pale, and she was concerned that his hands trembled slightly.

"So, how did it go tonight?" she asked.

Mark grinned. "About the same as it did for the cat that decided to pay a visit to Crufts."

"That bad," said Jennifer.

"I'm worried about him, Jen!" Mark declared suddenly. "You should have seen the anger in his eyes. It was frightening. I've never seen dad like that. And if we don't do something quick, God knows what will happen."

"That's why we wanted you to talk to him," said Jennifer, "and if you can't get him to see sense, no one can."

"Then we have to go through medical channels," said Mark, staring glumly into his cup."

"Have him sectioned, you mean?" Jennifer was horrified by the suggestion.

"Yes; if we have to. Look, Jen, what else can we do? We believe dad may be intending some time in the future to harm himself; maybe even mum. We can't just sit back and wait for it to happen."

"No; I won't believe that!" Jennifer said fiercely. "Dad would never harm mum. Even if he was completely out of his mind and planning to hurt himself he would never do anything like that. His love for her is just too strong. Somewhere deep down inside him I just know there must be something that will keep her safe no matter what."

Mark stared at his sister with a look that was so resolute, she held her breath. "He might if he believed he was taking her to a better life; a life she dearly wants, but lacks the courage to grasp."

"Oh, please, God, no," Jennifer whispered. Then her eyes filled with tears. "What's happening, Mark? A few days ago we were all happy; going on with our lives in the way we wanted. Now we're sitting here discussing having dad sectioned, and wondering if he will take it into his head to kill mum before we do?"

Mark placed his cup on the coffee table and put his arms around his sister, hugging her tight. "Look, Jen, it will be all right. We'll find a way around this. I'll have another chat with dad. Maybe I caught him on a bad day, and a crowded pub is hardly the place to have a proper discussion. You leave it with me. Now, what time does Pete get home from his shift?"

Jennifer glanced at the clock over the fireplace. "In half an hour, if the traffic is ok."

"Does he know what's going on?"

She shook her head.

"Then it's time he did. After all, he's your husband," Mark went on. "Talk it over with him. Doesn't he have a friend that works at one of the psychiatric hospitals?"

"Andrew Crampton," said Jennifer.

"That's him. Ask Pete to find out what's involved in having someone sectioned. Or maybe he might even know of a less drastic treatment: but for Christ sakes, make sure Pete doesn't let on he's making enquiries about dad. These things have a nasty way of getting back to the person in question."

"Oh Hell, I've just realized," Jennifer announced suddenly, jumping to her feet. "I have to get something finished for work tomorrow. There will be hell to pay if it isn't."

"I've got to get back myself," said Mark, standing also. Then he hugged his sister once more. "Don't let this nonsense with dad get to you, Jen. The Pemberton's have more determination in their little finger than any other family have in their whole body. When we put our minds together, why, we could solve the problems of the whole world."

Jennifer laughed and looked into her brother's eyes. "Course we can. Look out world, here come the Pembertons!"

Mark frowned. "Seriously though, Jen, I may not know what's got into dad, but I do know one thing; he's an intelligent man, and once he's made to understand how ridiculous this vision of his really is, and the effect it's having on his family, he'll snap out of it. "

"We said that before," Jennifer chided

"Yes we did, but a good idea is always worth repeating. Now, before you can say, objection, my Lord, everything will be back to normal."

Mark then gave his sister a quick peck on the cheek.

"See you, Jen," he said, heading for the door.

"Bye, Mark," said Jennifer, sending a sad smile after him.

That night in bed, Jennifer turned yet another page of the crime novel she was reading. Only half of her mind was on the rather weak plot of the seven hundred page hardback. The other half was working out the best moment to bring up the subject of her father, to her husband who was also propped up and reading a book.

She could tell by his rather serious expression that he was totally engrossed in the biography of Diana, Princess of Wales, and he might not appreciate being disturbed.

However, concluding that the welfare of his father-in-law must take priority over any book, she decide to inform him about what was going on. But she did have one fear. There were times during their six year marriage when she found Peter completely unreasonable in his opinions about certain subjects. He flatly refused to put a single coin in any collection box without ever explaining why. On the other hand he set up two direct debits of ten pounds a week to a children's charity, and a sanctuary for retired horses. He found all political parties equally corrupt, but would be willing to walk five miles through deep snow to vote for the Greens. And when it came to the environment, he wanted all the World's forests protected, no matter what the cost to their local inhabitants, but constantly complained that the fishing quota's for UK fishing boats should be increased.

Jennifer realized that she had no idea at all how her husband was going to react. It could just a easily be *'Nothing to do with us, darling; it's a private matter between your parents, so let's keep out of it, shall we,'* as *'That's terrible, darling. What can I do to help?'*

Jennifer closed her book and took a deep breath. Then she looked at Peter.

"Any good, darling?" she asked.

Peter smiled. "You wouldn't believe the things that went on in that place," he replied. "Seems that wealth and fame are no barrier to misery."

"I suppose not," said Jennifer. "Anyway, can I talk to you about something, darling?"

"Can't it wait until tomorrow?" Peter replied. "I'm in the middle of a conversation taking place between Diana and her butler."

"Don't worry; I'm sure they will still be talking when you get back to them," Jennifer quipped.

Peter placed a bookmark on the page he was reading; closed the book and placed it on his bedside table. Then he turned to face Jennifer. "Ok, so what is it you want to talk about?"

"It's dad," said Jennifer.

"Yours or mine?" said Peter.

"Mine," said Jennifer.

"So what's the problem?" said Peter. "Isn't he sleeping properly or something? Insomnia is common when people first retire."

"No, that's isn't it; or at least I don't think it is," said Jennifer. "It seems, according to mum, that he believes he had a visit from an angel last Sunday. Of course that in itself wouldn't be much of a problem, but he's also claiming that the angel has offered him and mum a second chance at being young again, but they have to die of some illness first, and he means in the near future; maybe only a few weeks from now."

"Naaa, nothing to worry about," Peter offered, picking up his book. "That's just one of those quirky waking-dreams everyone gets from time to time. I remember one I had about fifteen years ago. I knew I was awake because I could hear mum and dad having one of their middle-of-the-night chats, but my cat Oscar was sitting at the bottom of my bed, telling me about this mouse he let escape. I wasn't really listening to what Oscar was saying because I was working out how much money I could make from having the world's first talking cat."

"Then you woke up," said Jennifer.

"Well, we're not living in a mansion so I must have," Peter replied with a sigh.

"I'm being serious, you know," said Jennifer.

Peter put the book on his chest. "Ok, darling, let's have it. So dad really believes an angel came on a visit?"

"Yes."

"Mmmm, must have been quite a shock for him," said Peter, his expression serious"

"You can say that again," Jennifer replied.

"How is mum taking it?"

Jennifer tried to keep a tremble of panic out of her voice. "She's worried sick."

"Does she think he is suffering from some form of depression?" said Peter. "I've heard that depression can effect people's thoughts in all sorts of strange ways: some people lose the ability to speak, or even move their limbs, because of it."

"I suppose depression is a possibility," said Jennifer.

"Then he should visit his doctor," said Peter, "and the sooner the better. Sounds a bit serious to me if he's getting visions and his personality is changing. He's always been so practical and I would have expected him to laugh off something like that. The fact that he hasn't is definitely a reason for him to see someone about it."

Jennifer shook her head. "He refuses to talk about it to anyone but mum, and even then it always ends in a row."

Suddenly Jennifer burst into tears.

"Hey; hey!" Peter exclaimed, putting his arms around her. "There's no need to be upset, Jen. All we have to do is get him to see his GP, and I'm sure he can snap him out of it. Half the country are on anti-depressants. There's no shame in it these days."

"You don't understand," said Jennifer through her sobs. "Mum is worried that he might harm himself."

"Oh come on, darling; course he won't," said Peter, giving her a gentle shake. "I mean, except for this vision of his, he has been happy hasn't he?"

"I suppose so."

"Course he has. Now I don't want you worrying yourself. If I know John Pemberton, he'll soon get over whatever it is that's bothering him. And if he has to take a short course of medication to put him back on track, then that's no problem. I mean, nobody creates a fuss about such things these days. Everyone knows someone with depression. It's nearly as common as flu."

"But what if it's a very serious form of depression?" Jennifer suggested. "They can't cure everything with medication, you know?"

"There's always that possibility, of course," Peter conceded. "Now, I don't know very much about depression, but I think I heard somewhere that many people who do harm themselves have a long history of mood swings and difficult behaviour. I don't believe you can go to bed a contented man on a Saturday night, and wake up the following morning depressed and having thoughts about self-harming."

Jennifer wiped her eyes. "You don't know dad as well as I do. What's bothering us the most is that if he and mum don't get sick in the next few months, he might take matters into his own hands. Mum definitely believes he will."

"Hmm, that puts a different complection on the matter," Peter replied, frowning. "I think we should have some sort of meeting with the rest of the family to discuss it. I'll have a chat with Andrew Crampton tomorrow. I'm sure he will know what to do. He has probably seen just about every trick the brain can come up with when it's out of sorts."

Relief drove the tears from Jennifer's eyes. "Thanks, darling."

"No problem," said Peter, picking up the book again. "Now, I think I'll get back to Diana and her butler. God; who would be an employer these days!"

CHAPTER NINE

Friday 11th June

John took another plain biscuit from the biscuit barrel resting on his lap. He was sitting on the settee in the living-room and his feet were propped up on a stool. Beside him, Maggie watched the closing minutes of an old, black-and-white film. The subject of the film was murder and betrayal; not her favourite topic, but entertaining nevertheless.

She took a sip of her tea, and listened to the regular sound of munching as her husband ate his biscuit. He seemed content, and had been so for the last couple of days. She prayed with all her heart this would continue. But where was the contentment coming from? Was it due to a return to his old, care-free self, or a belief that a gift from God would soon be his?

John mentioned that he had met Mark for a drink in the pub, but refused to elaborate further. She could tell that it had not been a pleasant encounter, and decided to speak about it to her son at the first opportunity. However, that particular opportunity was finding it difficult to knock on her door. John was hanging around the house a great deal lately, as if waiting for something to happen; something he dare not miss. She had a terrible feeling she knew what it was.

John helped himself to another biscuit.

"That's eight, dear," Maggie scolded with a laugh.

"So what," came the curt reply. "They're cheap enough."

"I was only saying," said Maggie, concerned by the tone of the answer.

"I didn't realize I was being rationed," said John. "You should have told me."

Maggie flinched as she felt a chill creep towards her from her husband's body. She also felt a strong impulse to move away, but she fought against it.

"Don't be silly, dear. Of course you're not being rationed. It's just that I know you are proud of your figure; especially since most of your friends have run to seed. I don't want that to change."

John stared at his wife, his expression hard, almost hostile. "Very kind of you to worry about my pride, love. But the question is, do you worry about the sort of life I have?"

"What do you mean?" Maggie asked, confused.

"Surely the question is self-explanatory," said John. "Do you, or do you not worry about my life? For instance, does it matter to you how long I live? Do you care whether my life is full of fun and meaning, or just a long, slow decline into senility and death?"

"How can you ask me such a horrible question!" Maggie exploded. "Of course I worry about your health, and whether you are happy and fulfilled!"

"Well, it doesn't seem like that to me," said John, turning his attention back to the news that was just coming on.

"What are you talking about?" Maggie retorted. "I have devoted my entire life to you, and not once have I complained when things haven't gone as I expected."

"What things?" John demanded, staring at her once more.

"Just; things," said Maggie.

"Such as what?"

Maggie hesitated before answering. "Well, take that time when you decided to pull down the conservatory to allow more room for your flowers. I loved that conservatory: I used to sit out there and paint. In fact I could probably have lived there, it was so comfortable. The light coming in through the glass had a pure quality that only an artist or a photographer could really appreciate it. Yet I never said a single word of protest when you announced it had to go. And the time I wanted dusty pink carpets for downstairs, but you wanted pale blue, so pale blue they were. Well, it seems to me, John that, if anything, I worry about your needs just a little too much."

"Then you should have said at the time," John protested. "What good is it complaining after the changes have been made?"

"I'm not complaining!" Maggie shot back. "I'm just saying that; well; that sometimes you rush into these things without asking me how I feel about them."

"All those are just material things that can be easily changed," John grunted. "I'm talking about spiritual things; the needs of the spirit and the soul, if you like, not what stores have to offer."

"So we're back to your vision again, are we?" said Maggie. "All right then, let's say this angel is real, and he was sent by God to offer us a second chance of life. Have you for one single moment considered the ramifications of such an offer; have you?"

John's jawbone seemed to press tight against the flesh on his face; a sign that he was under pressure. "Of course I have," he replied in a low voice.

"Have you really," said Maggie, her tone condescending. "Then you must have come to terms with the fact that you will be younger than your own children; that they will die before you, which I understand for normal, decent people, is one of their worst nightmares. And answer me this, John, what will you tell the grandchildren when they ask you why their parents are going to get old and die before you? Oh, don't think they're too young for that. Modern children have a whole new conception that was totally beyond our capabilities when we were their age."

"I told you, I've considered all that," said John, suddenly on the defence. "What do you think, Maggie; that I've gone into this with my eyes shut. Well, you should know me by now. What do you think has been twisting my insides like they're going to snap. Of course I worry about the kids: they're my grandchildren, for God's sake!"

"And you're still going ahead with it!" Maggie cried. "My God, John, I never knew you could be so selfish."

"Selfish: so you want to grow old and die, do you?" John snapped. "Is that what you want; to slide slowly into oblivion; happy that your family will be there to see you planted six feet under the ground?"

Defiance flared in Maggie's eyes. "Yes, I am as a matter of fact. If God sees fit, then the both of us will leave our family behind. It's the way things are. It's the way things should be, and the idea of interfering in that natural process, well, it sickens me, if you must know."

"It sickens you, does it?" John shouted. "It's the way things are, and the way they should be?"

A terrible smile then appeared on his face, and he leaned closer to Maggie, almost threateningly. "Then, pray tell, love, who exactly do you think sent this angel to our room; because the last time I looked in the bible, angels only came to Earth on the instructions of God himself, or has there been a bit of rethinking in the higher echelons of the Church? Perhaps the devil is sending angels of his own, but then surely they would be dressed in black and floating upside-down?"

"No, it's not God, or the devil who sent you that vision," Maggie replied scathingly. "It's you, John; no one else. For some strange reason a deep-seated fantasy of yours has invaded our lives with destructive force and you refuse to do anything about it, and why, because it's what you want, and you're too selfish to even consider the possibility that you might need help."

"You only think that because the angel appeared to me and not you," John countered, "and do you know what, Maggie, I think you're jealous."

"Jealous!" Maggie exclaimed incredulously.

"Yes, jealous," said John, "because you have always been more religious than me. You often go to church, but I haven't set foot inside one for over five years. Yet, God sent the angel to me, and you think he should have chosen you. But I'm telling you hear and now, love, if he had, you would be whistling quite a different tune."

"I've had enough of this nonsense!" Maggie snapped, jumping to her feet. "Make whatever decision you like when that angel comes back, if he comes back, but leave me out of it. I want no part in this horrible fantasy of yours."

"You'll change your mind, love!" John shouted after her as she left the room. "See if you don't. Because when it comes down to it, all those morals of yours will go out the window when it's time for you to decide between them and being young again. And when that happens I hope you will apologize for trying to make me feel bad about it; about accepting a gift from God himself."

The sounds of heavy footsteps going up the stairs were the only reply.

Maggie broke two plates as she did the washing-up in the kitchen two hours after the argument with John. She was so angry that she forgot to use the dishwasher, and each mug was subjected to such aggressive drying that three of them finished up without handles.

The whole vision business was having a profound effect on her, and she couldn't even turn to her husband because he was the cause of her distress. She wasn't sure what was behind the vision, but she certainly resented him for bringing it into their almost idyllic lives. Before that night, they had been happy and enjoying their retirement. Now there seemed to be only talk about death and a terrible injustice that was about to be inflicted upon her family. Of course the vision was probably a figment of John's imagination, but deep down, she couldn't shake off the nagging doubt that he was right, and that God had indeed sent him a message. After all, who could say what was in the mind of God, and wasn't he supposed to work in mysterious ways. But the main reason for the doubt in her, despite the fact that it went against her belief in the way things were, was that for as long as she had known him, John Pemberton had rarely been that wrong about anything, and on the few occasions he had been wrong, a certain logic in his mistake was apparent. But if he was wrong about the vision, where was the logic?

Maggie heard her husband come into the kitchen, but she didn't turn round. She continued drying one of her three cast-iron saucepans with concentration that would have put a chess grandmaster to shame.

"I didn't mean to upset you, love," said John in a soft tone. "It's just that you don't seem to be on my side in this."

"That's because I'm not," Maggie replied coldly. "I've explained how I feel about it, and if you want to carry on without my support, then that's up to you."

John approached his wife and towered over her.

She felt his nearness but still didn't turn around. She could hear his deep breathing now, and when its intensity changed, she knew that his mood was changing too.

"Why are you behaving like this, love?" he pleaded. "We've been offered a wonderful gift and you want me to refuse it. No one in their right mind would pass up an opportunity to knock forty years of their age. Yet that's exactly what you're telling me to do. I mean, it's not as if we are taking the years from those we love. They won't lose anything, and who knows, maybe they will have the same offer when they reach our age."

Maggie put down the saucepan and turned to face her husband. Her expression was one of defiance and determination. "Now, you listen to me, John. I'm not telling you to stop doing whatever you really want to do, but I am telling you that I want no part of it, and you should respect my wishes the way I respect yours."

John suddenly grabbed her arms with strength that made her wince. "You say that, but what good is a fresh start to me without you?" he cried. "I don't want to go through this exciting experience alone. I want to share it with you. Is that so much to ask?"

Maggie pulled free, then smiled. "You know, John, when I first saw you, I thought you were the most handsome man I'd ever seen, that wasn't playing the lead in some Hollywood film. You were so tall, so, oh, I know this is a very old fashioned word these days, but I'm going to say it anyway, dashing; with your jet black hair and brown eyes, and that smile of yours; you should have to have some sort of government licence to walk around with a devastating smile like that. And when you wake up one morning, or however it will happen, looking just as you did when I first saw you, well, you will have young girls queuing up to ask you out, and I'll be happy for you, I really will, although it will break my heart."

" I don't want other women!" John exclaimed. "I want you."

"Then you have a decision to make, dear," said Maggie, with a dry smile. "You can have me here and now, or regress forty years and find someone else."

John turned suddenly and stormed out of the kitchen.

A few moments later Maggie heard the front door slam shut, and she burst into tears.

CHAPTER TEN

Saturday 12th June

"There must be some way around this!" Mark cried, his face distorted with frustration.

"Sorry, but there isn't," said Peter. "As I've already said, you can't just have someone sectioned. It's an extremely complicated procedure, involving his doctor and the authorities."

"But he could be dangerous. He might take it into his head to hurt himself and mum."

"That's your interpretation of the situation," said Peter, a frown on his thin face.

Mark's frustration turned to anger. "What the hell do you mean by that?"

"Look, Mark," Peter replied, "I'm on your side over this. But, honestly now, has John actually said he would hurt himself or Maggie?"

Mark's frustration rushed back and he pulled a face. "That's not the point. He might, and we have to do something before he does."

"Granted, but trying to have him sectioned is a complete waste of time. For instance, say you convinced John to discuss this vision with his GP. You know what some doctors are like these days. You have to walk into their surgery with your head tucked under your arm before they'll accept there just might be something seriously wrong with you. His GP will conclude that John has had a harmless hallucination after being woken up by some noise coming from outside the window, and another thing, John is his patient; he probably won't even discuss it with you."

"Then what can we do?"

"I'll get us all a drink," said Jennifer heading for her kitchen. She returned a few minutes later with two bottles of wine and four glasses.

Robert jumped from his seat to help her.

"You still haven't answered me?" Mark said to Peter.

Peter sighed and ran the fingers through his full head of chestnut hair. "This is not an easy problem at all to solve. How do we prevent someone from doing something they haven't said they will do in the first place, and if you do stop them, will it be enough?"

"How do you mean, darling?" said Jennifer as she handed out the drinks.

"Well, say we, oh, I don't know, kidnap John at the appropriate time? Didn't Maggie say that the angel told John that he must give his answer tonight?"

Jennifer nodded. "Early hours of tomorrow morning to be exact."

"So what if John misses his appointment with the angel because of some action we take?"

"That will be the finish of it," Mark offered cheerfully. "Oh, I suppose dad will be like an addict without his fix for a while, but you know dad, he can never hold a grudge for long, especially with his family. He'll calm down soon enough and forget that ridiculous vision of his."

"Yes, you could be right," said Peter in a much more subdued tone. "However, have you considered another possibility?"

Mark simply stared at his brother-in-law.

"John may regard our actions as moving the goal posts," Peter went on, "but can I just clarify one important point before we go any further with this There isn't any possibility that this vision is real, is there?"

Mark and Robert laughed out loud, but Jennifer just sipped her wine.

The laughter left Mark and he looked at his sister. "Jen?"

"How do I know whether someone's vision is real or not," she replied. "That question has been asked and unanswered for thousands of years. What do I know."

"This is ridiculous!" Mark shouted incredulously. "We're sitting here, in the twenty first century, trying to decide whether our father should be allowed to act on a vision he's had, not to mention that it may be nothing more than a dream of, course. After all, he even admitted himself that he was asleep before he saw the vision."

"He says he was awake when the vision arrived because it woke him up and he would know the difference," said Jennifer. "He may have an incredibly imaginative mind, but it's a disciplined one. He could tell the difference, I'm certain he could."

"Then you believe him?"

Jennifer stared back at her brother. "As a matter of fact I do."

"I need another drink," Mark groaned, reaching for a bottle. "Nothing is making any sense to me sober."

"What's changed your mind, Jen?" Robert asked.

Jennifer shrugged. "Nothing I can define enough to put into words. I suppose it must be my belief in dad. I don't think he would allow his mind to cause all this trouble simply over some fantasy; he's far too focused for that."

Robert finished his drink and concentrated his attention on Peter. "You were saying something about our actions moving the goal posts?"

Peter looked suddenly uncomfortable. "I'm not sure I should say, not after what Jen has just said. I don't want to upset her."

Jennifer smiled warmly at her husband. "That's all right, darling. You carry on. We're here to discuss the matter, not keep things from one another."

"All right then," said Peter, "just for a moment, let's assume that this vision of John's is simply a fantasy created by his mind. In that case, what's to stop his mind doing it again if we prevent him from seeing the angel tonight?"

"My God," said Mark, shocked, "I never thought of that. He could see this angel next week, or the week after, even next year, and we wouldn't know about it if he decided not to tell us, and would he if we interfered now?"

"I would say that not telling us is a foregone conclusion," said Robert, "especially if we succeed in having him locked up for a bit."

"I think it's a real possibility that he will have the vision again," said Peter, knowingly. "After all, it must be based on some pretty powerful needs to make him act the way he has been lately."

"Then I'm moving back in," Mark announced.

"With mum and dad?" said Robert, clearly surprised.

"Why not," said Mark. "I don't have a family, and mum and dad have always said there was a bed there for me any time I liked."

"Well, it won't be there now," Robert replied. "Dad will be on to you in a second. He's not a fool, you know."

"We have to try something," Mark protested. "Every time my phone has rang lately I've nearly jumped out of my skin, and the nightmares I've had, believe me, you don't want to hear about them!"

"I think we should wait until after Sunday," said Jennifer. "Dad told mum that they won't get sick for a couple of months. We should back off and let everyone calm down for a while. I'm going to give mum a ring and advise her to go along with dad. Otherwise, all this arguing may bring everything forward, and that's the last thing we want."

"Good idea, Jen," said Robert. "We'll keep an eye on things, but no more family meetings for now or dad will get suspicious; agreed?"

"I suppose so," said Mark, clearly undecided.

"Excellent," said Robert. "Now come on, Jen, how about one of your famous ham-and-cheese sandwiches. I'm starving."

"Anyone else?" Jennifer asked.

"Just ham for me," said Mark, "and with a bit of pickle if you have any."

"Pete?"

"Not for me, darling. I had something earlier."

Jennifer vanished into the kitchen, and Peter helped himself to another drink. There was a new look on his face; a look of worry.

"What's up, Pete?" said Robert.

Peter shrugged. "Nothing special, just a little concerned about Jen. You know, last night she told me she didn't believe in John's angel. Then she said she did. And she changed her mind at least a dozen times after that. It's as if there are two forces inside her; each battling for dominance, and what with the pressure of work and all, it could be too much for her."

"Aaa you're worrying about nothing," Mark laughed. "Jen's Margaret Thatcher when it comes to toughness. It's one of the main requirements if you want to be a barrister."

"You could have chosen a more complementary metaphor," Peter grinned, "but I appreciate what you're saying."

"We're all in this together, Pete," said Robert. "No one is going to be allowed to shoulder more of the responsibility than they can handle. Jen will be ok; we'll see that she is."

Peter nodded. "Thanks, Rob, I needed to hear that."

CHAPTER ELEVEN

Sunday 13th June

Maggie opened her eyes with a start. She was lying on her right side, and without moving, stared at the clock on the bedside table.

The time was 3:15am.

She silently chastised herself. She had fallen asleep despite her resolve to stay awake, and to make matters worse, she had turned over. How could she have been so foolish. If her husband was being visited by angels, she just had to see for herself.

She could hear John speaking softly in the bed beside her, but no matter how hard she tried, she couldn't make out what he was saying. His voice was very low, but its emotional content was almost tangible in its intensity.

Fortunately there was a glow coming through the netted window, and she could just make out John's reflection in the dressing table mirror. He was sitting up straight, and so still in the soft light that she could easily imagine he was a ghostly painting in an invisible frame, hanging on an invisible wall. Somehow she knew he was pale and in some sort of dream-like state.

She raised her head very slowly and turned to look in the direction her husband was focusing his attention. There was nothing there but an old bow-fronted oak chest of drawers with a small photo of John's great, great grandfather who was famous in the eighteen hundreds for discovering something to do with the weaving industry.

Maggie felt frustration raging inside her. She so desperately wanted to shake her husband and force him to see that there was no angel in the room, only his imagination responding to his desires, and creating havoc in the process. But she wasn't a psychiatrist, and didn't they say that to waken someone who was sleepwalking could be dangerous? So was she to leave him, talking to an imaginary angel; talking their future and very lives away. How could she bear it?

Then an idea came to her.

She placed her head on her pillow once more and took a deep breath.

"John?" she whispered as softly as she could.

Her husband continued speaking.

"John dear?" she whispered a little louder.

Again no change.

"John dear?"

John stopped talking.

The silence hit Maggie like the unwelcome touch of a ghost and she held her breath. Her heart began to race in dreadful anticipation. Would her interruption anger him? Had she just made matters worse?

Then she felt John lay back on his pillow, and when soft snores followed, she went back to sleep with tears of sadness in her eyes.

John munched noisily on his cornflakes whilst he read the morning paper. Maggie watched every move he made as intently as a weasel does a rabbit. 'When is he going to tell me?' The words burned in her brain like a branding iron. Once again he was up before her and had laid the table, but whereas last time he was clearly under some terrible strain, now he was calmness personified. He had kissed her good morning with a full smile on his face; asked her to be seated, and then poured cornflakes from the box into her bowl: milk and sugar followed. She wasn't sure yet whether this unusual behaviour was something to be concerned about. There had been an uneasy truce between them since he had stormed out of the kitchen, and now he was acting as if all was well in the world.

"John?" she said.

Her husband stopped munching and stared back at her. "Yes, love?"

"About last night?" Maggie carried on when she saw no anger surface.

He smiled. "What about it, love?"

"The angel you were expecting; did he come?"

John nodded, the smile still on his face.

"What did you tell him?"

"Don't worry about it, love. It's been sorted out," said John, with happiness clear in his voice and manner.

"Has it?"

"It's all cushty, as Del Boy would say, love. Now, all we have to do is wait."

Maggie's heart missed a beat. "Wait for what, dear?"

A slight frown creased John's forehead. "The disease, of course. You seem very forgetful lately, love. Are you feeling all right?"

"I'm fine," said Maggie, "but the angel; are you absolutely sure he called last night?"

"Well, if it wasn't him, who was I talking to? Of course he came last night. You're just being silly now."

Maggie braced herself to say what she must say, even though she was risking a confrontation. "I have a confession

The Colour of the Young

to make, dear. I hope you don't mind, but I was awake when you were talking to the angel."

"Nonsense!" John laughed. "You were snoring away like you always do, and don't try and deny that women snore, because I saw a TV programme on the subject. Women snore nearly as often as men, but men snore louder: something about having bigger lungs."

"No, I wasn't going to deny that I snore, dear," said Maggie. "In fact, I've woken myself up on quite a few occasions when I've been particularly loud. But I was awake last night. I dropped off for a while, but I did wake up when you were talking to the angel."

John frowned. "Then why did you ask me if he came? It's too early in the morning for games, love."

"I just wanted to be sure that you saw him," Maggie replied.

John's frown remained for a moment; then it vanished and his eyes brightened with pleasure. "So you saw him as well! This is fantastic, love. Why didn't you say something? I'm sure he wouldn't have minded you joining in. After all, it concerns you as well."

Maggie shifted uncomfortably in her chair, but there was no going back now. She had committed herself.

"Well, love?" John prompted.

"The reason I didn't join in, dear, is because, well, because I didn't see anyone there."

John's expression reflected his confusion. "You didn't?"

"No, dear, I didn't."

John turned his attention back to his paper for a moment. Then he looked at her again, and the smile returned. "How stupid of me, love!" he exclaimed. "Of course you didn't see him. He was my vision, not yours, so obviously it was exclusively mine. Don't fret about it, though, love, it won't make any difference. This gift is for the both of us. Anyway, as if I would accept it without you. What would be the point in that."

"Oh," said Maggie. "Yes, I do see that now, dear. The vision was yours, and only you could see it."

"That's it, love. Sorry. Anyway, I told him that we are ready for the next development, so it shouldn't be very long now."

"You mean the illness?"

"Yes, the illness," John replied impatiently. Then he laughed. "Honestly, love, I think this offer has come along just in time. Otherwise you would be worrying me by now. You're certainly not as sharp as you used to be."

"So, you have accepted this offer on my behalf, despite my aversion to it?" Maggie inquired evenly.

"Of course I have," said John, clearly unperturbed. "After all, you already told me to accept: don't you remember?"

"Yes, I suppose I did, didn't I," Maggie admitted with some reluctance.

"Yes, love, you did, but there's no need to worry yourself about it. You don't have to go through with it if you don't want to, but I had to take into consideration that you might change your mind later, so I accepted for you, just in case. Anyway, I know for a fact you'll come round, love. I mean, what woman could resist being young again. The huge amounts of money women spend on creams and make-up speaks for itself, don't you think?"

"After we die from the illness, what then?" Maggie asked. "Do we wake up the next morning as a young couple?"

John shook his head. "I don't know, love."

"Didn't you ask?" said Maggie, surprised by the answer. "Surely you're interested in that aspect of the process?"

John scowled. "There's no need to take that tone with me, love, and for your information I did ask, but I didn't get a reply, so I didn't ask again. I don't know how these things work, but I suspect it isn't a good idea to make demands of any angel sent by God. Now, if you don't mind, I'm trying to finish my breakfast."

CHAPTER TWELVE

Sun 13th June

Maggie arrived at her daughter's house in Harrow at 4:30pm.

She paused to admire the three bedroom detached property and felt a sense of pride despite the seriousness behind her visit. She always knew that Jennifer was going to be the great achiever in the family, and by the looks of it she was well on the way. The house was in the Mock Tudor style, like many in the street, and the front garden, a bricked drive with small flower borders, was also mirrored elsewhere.

She usually enjoyed opening the fancy, wrought-iron gate and walking up to the solid oak front door which had beautiful, leaded, stained glass positioned as a fan above it.

A nervous tremor took hold of her as she rang the bell.

Seconds later Jennifer opened the door and Maggie stepped inside.

Jennifer took her mother's coat and hung it on a brass hook as Maggie made her way into the living-room.

Jennifer followed her in and they both sat on the leather settee.

"I do wish you had let me collect you instead of you having to get the train," Jennifer protested.

"It isn't a long journey, dear," said Maggie, "and the walk from the station gave me time to think. Anyway, I've been stuck in that house rather a lot lately. John seems contented to spend most of his time in the garden, and I don't like to leave him for any length of time."

The Colour of the Young

"He hasn't that kind of illness?" Jennifer prosted. "Surely you can leave him on his own once in a while?"

"He may not be physically sick, dear," said Maggie, "but he certainly isn't himself. Anyway, I only worry when he is on his own."

"I suppose so," Jennifer replied. Then she transfixed her mother. "Right, mom, let's have it. I promised Mark and Robert that I would let them know immediately I found out, and if they're feeling anywhere near as nervous as me, then I feel sorry for them."

Maggie sighed. "I'm afraid the angel did visit last night, dear."

Jennifer also let out a sigh, but it was long and slow. "Right, so the problem obviously hasn't gone away. Pity; I hoped it was a one-off."

"So did I, " Maggie agreed. "There's something else."

Jennifer's brow furrowed. "Oh?"

"I'm afraid I was awake when your father was speaking to the angel, and -"

"Oh my God, you saw him too?" Jennifer interrupted, shocked at the idea.

"That's just the point," Maggie replied evenly. "There was no one there; no angel, nothing at all, but your father was sitting up in bed talking and listening."

"God, whatever you do, don't tell him," Jennifer warned. "You never know what he will do if you prove to him it was all just a dream."

"Too late for that," Maggie replied. "I told him at breakfast."

Eyes wide with concern, Jennifer put her hand to her mouth. "Oh, mom, you didn't! How did he react?"

Maggie smiled. "Well, for a moment he was confused: then he said that of course I wouldn't see the angel because it was his vision, not mine. And I was not to worry about it as he gave the answer for both of us."

Jennifer visibly relaxed. "How considerate of him. So, what happens next?"

Maggie shrugged. "To be perfectly honest, I'm not quite sure. I don't think there will be any more visits from angels, and I'm hoping that everything will settle down now. But -"

"You are still worried," Jennifer finished. "So, come on, mom, what else is there?"

Maggie gave a strained laugh. "Oh, I'm just being silly, dear. You see, I have always trusted your father's instincts, and I can't help feeling, deep down, that he wouldn't behave like this if there wasn't something in it. I don't mean angels and messages, of course, but something."

"That's only natural in a marriage like yours," said Jennifer, smiling warmly. "The trouble is it does leave you rather vulnerable to this sort of thing, I'm afraid, mum."

Maggie looked puzzled. "How so?"

"Well," said Jennifer cautiously as she didn't want to offend her mother, "you see dad as being perfect; or perhaps not exactly perfect, but nearly so; right?"

"I suppose I do," said Maggie.

Encouraged by her mother's agreement, Jennifer carried on. "And thinking so highly of his opinions and his decision-making, it would be quite understandable if you might have forgotten that he is only a human being like the rest of us, therefore, when he does make a humongous mistake, as we all do at some time or another, you may be inclined to; how can I put this, convince yourself that he must be right and the rest of us wrong."

Maggie frowned with indignation. "Don't be silly, dear!" she exclaimed. "I never said your father couldn't make a mistake: that's ridiculous. Of course he can be wrong about things like anyone else."

"You say that, mum, but deep down you don't believe it," Jennifer replied, "and it's very important that you are fully aware of dad's frailties."

A scathing laugh shot from Maggie, and she squared her shoulders "Nonsense. I have been married to John for over forty years, so you couldn't possibly tell me anything about your father I don't already know. Anyway, why are you talking to me like this; what's on your mind?"

"If you must know, mum," Jennifer replied, "I'm just as worried about your behaviour as dad's."

"My behaviour!" Maggie cried. "What on Earth would make you say something like that? Your father is the one getting visions. All I have done is go to my children for help: what's so strange about that?"

"Of course there isn't anything wrong with asking for our help," Jennifer protested. "That's not what I meant, mum. What I meant is that despite all you have told us about dad's visions, I detect a certain -"

"A certain what?" Maggie asked when Jennifer suddenly fell silent.

"A certain, acceptance," said Jennifer.

"I most certainly do not accept any of your father's behaviour," Maggie declared, "and I have to say, Jennifer, I find your attitude almost as disturbing as John's. I came round here to ask your advice, and instead you accuse me of all sorts. First of all you tell me I think of your father as some sort of god-like figure, which I don't even if I do believe him to be in the right over most things. Then you accuse me of accepting his ridiculous behaviour, which I obviously don't since I'm here in your house trying to find some way to stop it. Well, obviously I have caught you on a bad day, so if you don't mind I'll be getting back."

Maggie stood up, and alarmed, Jennifer grabbed her right hand. "Don't go, mum!" she pleaded. "Please, sit down, will you. I'm sorry, I didn't make my meaning clear. You have it all wrong."

Reluctantly Maggie sat back in her seat, but refused to look at her daughter.

"I'm really sorry, mum," said Jennifer, close to tears, "it's the barrister in me. I see a problem and I go straight at it like an arrow towards a bull's-eye, and I suppose I forget that I might be charging straight through people's feelings: but I don't mean to, honestly. Will you forgive me; please, mum?"

For a few moments Maggie's expression remained stern. Then she looked at her daughter and smiled. "It's all right, dear, I know you are trying to help. Perhaps I am being a bit over-sensitive. This whole business is starting to get to me, and no matter what argument I try with your father to give up this nonsense, he either counters it with a better one, or simply tells me that I'm wrong. Whatever I do I can't seem to win with him."

Jennifer tightened her grip on her mother's hand. "Oh, look, mum, we're all on your side, and now that dad has given his answer to the angel, I think it would be best not to confront him any more. Up to now there was a deadline and he was under pressure. Surely he should be able to relax for a while. I mean, how is his mood when the two of you are not arguing?"

"I suppose he is contented," Maggie admitted, her smile fading, "but then why wouldn't he be. After all *'Job done!'* as far as he is concerned."

"Surely that's good, isn't it?" said Jennifer. "I mean, assuming he doesn't intend to do anything silly, how long will he have to wait to get sick; years probably?"

Maggie frowned. "Oh, certainly not years, dear. Your father would never wait that long. Weeks, or even months, perhaps, but certainly not years. No, he will reassess the situation after what he considers a suitable length of time has passed."

"We'll settle for that," said Jennifer. "Let him reassess as much as he wants. All we need is time to come up with a plan. Dad caught us out on this occasion: next time we'll be ready for him; you'll see."

"I certainly hope so," said Maggie.

"You bet!" Jennifer declared, her eyes reflecting her excitement of fighting a good fight. Then the excitement left her eyes to be replaced by concern. "Just one thing, mum," she continued in a soft but resolute tone, "you won't give in to dad, will you? You won't stop resisting him? Oh, I don't mean arguing or disagreeing with him all the time. That would make life impossible for you both. No, I mean deep inside you, you will keep your own beliefs alive? Some terrible change has taken place inside dad's head, and you must never allow him to pass that on to you. Dad needs you to be strong, mum, even if he doesn't know it at the moment. You must stay focused for the both of you, and try not to worry too much. We'll sort this out."

"Of course, dear," said Maggie, smiling and touching her daughter's face. "You must not worry too much, either."

CHAPTER THIRTEEN

Friday 18th June

Maggie smiled as she watched her husband through the kitchen window. He was kneeling by one of the flower beds, loosening the soil with a miniature fork. John's love of flowers started when he used to help his father in the garden when he was a child, and no matter what the weather, he would be out there, always managing to find something to do, even when it was raining. A long time ago Maggie had learned that there was no point in protesting when his green fingers began throbbing. It was nature calling to him and he must answer, though the sky be sending a deluge to quench the ever-present thirst of the soil.

Maggie returned her attention to the small amount of washing-up in the sink.

Then a loud retort from John drew her attention once more.

She watched as he flexed the fingers of his right hand a few times, before picking up the fork he had dropped. And when he dropped it again and began flexing his fingers once more, she became concerned enough to investigate.

"What's the matter, dear?" she asked as she approached across the fine-cut lawn.

John threw an angry expression at her. "Nothing!" he grunted. "Just my blasted hand playing up again. Must be a touch of rheumatism or worse still, arthritis. At least I won't have to worry about taking any tablets if it is."

"Why don't you come inside and rest for a while," Maggie offered. "You look tired. "

"I've only been out here for half an hour," John replied, now rubbing his right hand with his left, "and I'm not tired. I have a headache, that's all."

"Please, dear, just for a little while," Maggie begged. "I'm worried about you. Come in and sit down. I'll make us both some tea. Anyway, it looks like it's going to rain soon: the air feel's damp and it could be affecting your joints. You can always come out later if you want."

"I'm all right, Maggie!" John retorted. "Now let me get on with this, will you. The blasted weeds are everywhere."

"All right, dear," Maggie sighed. "I'll leave you to carry on, but don't overdo it. After all, you have all the time in the world now that you are retired."

"Just so long as you stop fussing," John grumbled, returning to the weeds.

Maggie watched him for a few moments, shocked at how quickly a good mood could turn bad.

Then she left him to it.

CHAPTER FOURTEEN

Wednesday 23rd June

"Who were you chatting to all that time on the phone?" John asked cheerfully as he walked into the living-room. "Good thing I prepared well for our retirement or British Telecom would be threatening to cut us off by now."

Maggie smiled back as she sat on the settee. "Alison phoned to tell me about their holiday in Greece. They had a fantastic time, and even met a couple of people from London."

John dropped into the armchair opposite and stretched out his long legs. "I hate it when that happens. All they do is go on about what a good time they're having and preventing you from having one. There should be a law against that sort of thing."

"Don't be silly, dear," said Maggie. "I think it's nice to meet English people abroad. It makes me feel safer somehow; not so far from home."

"That's because you're obviously insecure when you're away from here," said John.

"Perhaps," said Maggie. "Anyway, I've invited them to dinner on Friday at eight."

John bent down and slipped off his shoes without comment.

This silence concerned Maggie. "You don't mind, do you?"

John leaned back in his chair, with a long sigh. "Mind what, love?"

"About inviting Alison and Patrick to dinner?"

"Course not," said John, staring at his wife. "Why should I mind?"

Maggie hesitated. "Well; it's just that you don't seem to be in the mood lately for visitors."

"Yes I am," John replied, frowning. "I haven't asked you not to invite anyone, have I?"

"No; but I couldn't help noticing that Jimmy doesn't call for you on Monday's like he used to. At one time you could set your watch by the time he rang the bell at seven."

John shrugged. "Aaaa; that's nothing, love. Jimmy always liked going to the darts match at The Fox more than I did: never could see the point of throwing small bits of pointed metal at a round board for half the night. A game like that only encourages people to drink far more than they should."

Maggie was puzzled. "I didn't know you felt like that. So why did you go then?"

John shrugged again. "Jimmy was a friend so I just tagged along."

Maggie was still puzzled. "Why did you say he *was* a friend?"

John's expression soured. "Was; is, what does it matter."

"Well, one means past and the other means present," said Maggie.

John made no comment, but settled further into his chair.

"Have you two fallen out?" Maggie asked, concern putting an edge to her voice.

"No, love, we haven't fallen out."

"But he doesn't call anymore?"

"Look," said John firmly, "some friendships last and some don't, it's as simple as that."

"So you have fallen out?"

A exasperated sigh shot from John. "If you must know, we decided to call it a day; satisfied now?"

"I see," said Maggie. "So who's decision was that?"

"Both of us."

"When did you both decide this, and who suggested it first?"

John's eyes narrowed with suspicion. "What do you mean?"

"I mean, were you walking to the pub, were you in the pub, or were you walking home from the pub when the decision to end the friendship was made? And who said it first?"

John's fists clenched. "Look, Maggie, why are you asking me all these stupid questions?"

"Because Jimmy has been your friend for nearly ten years," said Maggie, "and suddenly he isn't anymore, at least not since -"

"Not since what?"

"Not since you had your vision', and I was just wondering if you told him about it."

Her husband's face turning pale told Maggie that her suspicions and fears were justified.

"That's private, family business!" John snapped, jumping to his feet. "Why would I discuss it with an outsider?"

And before Maggie could reply, John stormed from the room and thumped up the stairs.

She decided not to follow.

CHAPTER FIFTEEN

Friday 25th June

Maggie quickly made her way to the front door and opened it.

Alison and Patrick Stebbings stepped into the hall and kissed her on the cheek.

"How was the journey?" Maggie inquired, closing the door.

"Oh, the usual game of dodgems with the drivers from hell," Alison quipped, taking off her coat and hanging it on a wall hook. "I suppose it stops me getting bored and nodding off at the wheel."

"You never stop talking long enough to nod off," said Patrick, smirking as he hung his jacket next to his wife's.

"For that little gem of wisdom, darling," said Alison, "you can do the driving home."

"You know very well I hate driving at night," Patrick protested with genuine concern.

"Precisely," said Alison, throwing a wink at Maggie.

Then she and Patrick followed Maggie into the living-room.

John quickly left his armchair to greet his sister-in-law and her husband.

"I swear you're taller every time I see you, John," said Alison. "Surely you can't still be growing?"

"Probably all those hormones in the meat I eat," said John. "Maybe I should go vegetarian."

Alison laughed and sat on the settee.

Patrick sat next to her, smiling all over his face. He loved these visits to Alison's family far more than he let on to anyone. Being the only offspring of over-possessive parents, he grew from being a lonely child into a lonely teenager. And at the age of twenty-six, just when he had resigned himself to an equally lonely adulthood, he met Alison, and his life changed forever. Now, at the age of sixty-two, with his own financial consultancy, and accepting Alison's family as his own, he couldn't be happier.

Patrick wasn't particularly tall for a man; standing a little over five feet eight. And his grey, receding hair, thin nose, wide mouth, small eyes and pointed chin robbed him of any good looks. But what he lacked in appearance he more than made up for in a cheerful disposition. Everyone meeting him for the first time felt instantly at ease in his company, and it was this quality that first attracted Alison who was almost an identical copy of Maggie, though two inches taller and three years younger.

"How is retirement suiting you?" Patrick said to John as he sat back down.

"So-so," John replied.

"Red or white wine anybody?" Maggie asked suddenly.

"Red for us," said Alison.

"Same here, love," said John.

"So-so doesn't sound too promising after all the years of preparing for it?" said Patrick.

John shrugged. "Yes, well, there are no guarantees in this life, Pat; you, of all people, should know that."

"Of course," Patrick replied, "but retirement doesn't carry the same risks as the financial markets, John. When you retire you are in control, not the whims of other people and their pockets."

John's face was hard as he stared back. "Retirement isn't only about money, you know. There are other forces at work to give you sleepless nights."

Pat frowned. "What forces?"

"You'll find out when you retire."

"Me; retire," Pat exclaimed with a laugh, "no thank you very much! My harness fits me very well and I'm happy wearing it for many years to come."

"If you're allowed to," said John.

Maggie walking into the room with a silver tray containing two bottles of French wine and four glasses, prevented Patrick from replying, but he was disturbed by John's negative mood. Had something happened between him and Maggie; he desperately hoped not.

For a few moments Maggie played hostess before finally sitting in her armchair. The smile on her face was strained because she had caught the tail-end of the conversation between her husband and Patrick. And the ending of the long friendship between John and Jimmy was still fresh in her mind. Involving even more people in their problems now would be more than she could stand.

"You were saying about other forces?" said Patrick to John. "Care to elaborate?"

John opened his mouth to reply, but Maggie got in first.

"Will you just listen to those two, Alison!" she exclaimed. "I arrange a nice, cosy dinner for us and the men treat it like some question-and-answer session. No wonder there are so many men in politics, which wouldn't be a bad thing of they talked sense."

"Sorry, Maggs," said Patrick sheepishly. "I was only showing an interest."

"That's all right, Pat," said Maggie. "Don't take any notice of John; it's early days yet; he's still trying to find his feet."

John gave his wife an unfriendly glance, but said nothing.

An hour later they were seated at a rectangular, solid oak table, standing in the middle of the dining room, which was decorated in red wallpaper with gold fleur-de-lis. A large, mahogany bookcase containing John's collection of first edition crime novels stood in one corner of the room, and a number of prints of racing horses from the nineteenth century adorned the walls. A small crystal chandelier suspended from a ceiling rose, and a parquet flooring completed the sixties appearance of the room.

"Mmmm; lovely," said Alison tasting the meat on her plate. "What is it, Maggs?"

"I think it's called chicken, my love," Patrick quipped, sitting next to his wife.

"I know it's chicken, you fool!" Alison declared, giving him a playful dig in the side with her elbow. "I was talking about what the chicken was cooked in."

"It's in a white wine sauce with herbs and garlic," Maggie explained. "I wish I could say I made it myself, but that new Italian store in Hadley Street is responsible, I'm afraid."

"No problem," said Alison. "After all, who needs homemade when shop-bought tastes like this. I would be quite happy to dump our cooker, but Pat just has to have his beef stew made from only fresh ingredients and simmered in the oven, for three hours, would you believe."

"Haven't you ever heard of slow cooking to bring out the flavour of the meat?" Patrick protested.

"Haven't you ever heard of Global Warming?" Alison shot back. "I think they should take your preference for cooking the traditional way into consideration when agreeing to levels of carbon emissions."

"Now the conversation has become far too techinal for me," said Patrick. "So, how about you, Maggs, is having a hubby under one's feet all day long as painful an experience as we are led to believe?"

Maggie smiled. "I better say no or John could claim the same about me. After all, I'm retired too, you know."

"United in misery, eh," said Patrick, laughing.

"Pat!" Alison scolded.

"It's all right, Alison," said John with a forced smile. "Your husband is just having a joke; isn't that right, Pat?"

Pat hesitated before answering, rather taken back at the fact that he was the only one who had laughed. "Course I am, folks. You all know me; subtle as a lump of concrete and as funny as a hyena."

"How's the job coming along, Alison?" Maggie asked when an awkward silence followed Patrick's remark.

"Oh, not too bad at the moment," said Alison. "The takeover is just about complete and except for a few new faces around the office, everything's more or less as it was. The general consensus is that the new owners will eventually bring fresh money and vitality to the company. And I must admit, everything was getting a bit staid before they came along. We may have been one of the most forward-thinking, fashion wholesalers in the country at one time, but these days you can't rest on your laurels. You have to be right at the heart of things, fighting the way you would when you were first starting out, and it's been a few years since Swavenad has done much of that."

"Mean-and-keen, I suppose," John offered, staring at his plate.

"It's the only way," Alison replied.

Suddenly there was a clatter, and such was the growing tension in the room, that everyone jumped.

"Sorry about that," said John, quickly wiping white sauce from the front of his shirt with a Irish linen serviette. "Stupid knife slipped out of my hand."

"Want me to get you a clean shirt, dear?" said Maggie.

"There's only a few spots," John replied. "Maybe it will give Alison a few ideas for a new Splashed Range."

"Stranger things have happened," said Alison, feeling awkward.

Maggie reached over with her serviette to wipe a spot her husband had missed.

"I can manage!" he snapped. "Stop fussing, will you. I'm not an invalid."

Shocked and embarrassed by the rebuke, Maggie returned to her meal.

After that, no more was said until they left the table and returned to the living-room. And after two hours of genial chat, it was time for Maggie and John's guests to leave.

It was 11.30pm.

Five minutes into their drive home to Highgate, Alison couldn't stand the silence in the BMW any longer. Patrick was the talker, yet he was strangely quiet.

"You're not saying much, darling?" she said.

"Just thinking," said Patrick.

"About what?"

"About the tension at your sister's tonight."

Alison gave a dry smile. "Trouble in paradise, you mean?"

"There's no need to be flippant about it," Patrick scolded. "It would have taken a power-saw to cut through the atmosphere in that house. Something must be wrong."

Alison sighed, turning the car left into Grange Street. "The trouble with you, Pat is that you expect far too much from Maggie and John."

Pat stared at his wife, frowning. "What do you mean?"

"Well," said Alison, "you're always going on about how wonderful they are; the perfect family."

"It's true, isn't it," said Patrick. "They are obviously devoted to one another, and their kids are great. To my mind that is a perfect family."

"And you desperately want to be a part of it," said Alison.

"What's wrong with that?" Patrick asked, turning his attention back to the road in front. It was a beautiful night for driving; dry, with very little traffic about, but he wasn't in the mood to enjoy it.

"There's nothing wrong with it," Alison replied. Then her expression displayed her feeling of pity for her husband. "Look, darling, I know you had a very lonely childhood, and your adult life wasn't much better before you met me. And I know you wanted kids of your own, and I'm sorry I couldn't give them to you because of that botched abortion I had when I was sixteen. But you can't expect Maggie and John to provide a family for you; it's not fair on them."

"Don't be silly," Patrick protested indignantly. "I expect no such thing."

"Oh yes you do," said Alison. "You know very well you would visit them every week if I let you, so don't bother denying it. Now, even perfect families have their down times. Maybe they had an argument just before we arrived. It does happen, you know, even in the best of marriages."

"An argument about what?" Patrick asked.

Alison gave an exasperated sigh. "For heaven's sake, darling, I don't know! Maybe it was something to do with

Mark. Or maybe Maggie gave one of John's favourite jumpers away to the charity shop during one of her clearouts. All I'm trying to say is that they are normal people, so naturally they row about things, and some of our visits are bound to coincide with those rare occasions."

"What about that business with the knife?" Patrick asked stiffly.

"Oh, you mean the way John snapped at Maggie. That's probably because he was still angry from their argu -"

"Before he snapped at her," Patrick interrupted. "When he dropped the knife; did you see, because I certainly did?"

Alison frowned. "See what; that he dropped the knife? What's unusual about that: we all get clumsy as we grow older?"

"He didn't just drop it. I mean he did drop it, but just before he did, his hand was shaking."

"How do you mean, shaking?"

"Shaking; trembling, and it was then that the knife dropped."

"I didn't notice that," said Alison. "So what was the cause; was he that angry?"

Patrick's thin face was rock-hard. "It wasn't anger. I'm sure I've heard of it before; something to do with the signals from the brain not getting through properly."

"Oh, now you're just jumping to conclusions," Alison berated.

"No I'm not," said Patrick. "There's definitely something medically wrong with him."

"Then why didn't you say anything?"

A grunt shot from Patrick. "With the mood he was in; no thank you very much! Couldn't you give Maggie a ring and talk to her about it?"

"What, and tell her that you think he has something wrong with his brain?" Alison chided. "You must be joking."

"No, of course not," said Patrick. "You don't have to be that blunt about it. All you have to do is tell her we noticed, and suggest he sees a doctor. You don't need to mention anything about his brain: just point out that he might have a trapped nerve in his neck; that's a common problem, though I think it's more serious with John."

Convinced that her husband was overreacting, Alison nevertheless gave into his fears. "All right, darling, I'll give Maggie a ring tomorrow. But in my opinion you're creating a fuss about nothing."

"Maybe I am," said Patrick, clearly relieved, "but it's always better to be safe than sorry with things like this. And if it does turn out to be just a trapped nerve, Maggie will still appreciate our concern."

CHAPTER SIXTEEN

Tuesday 29th June

Maggie sat in the waiting room of her local surgery. Usually a calm person during visits, she couldn't help fretting on this occasion due to her uncertainty. In some ways John was a very private person, and she could just imagine how he would feel if he could see her now, preparing to go behind his back: angry certainly, and worst of all, betrayed. Because wasn't that what people did when they betrayed someone, confide in an outsider that which should be private. But she couldn't help herself. As well as loyalty, didn't she also have a duty of care to her husband, and if his mental faculties had been compromised somehow, wasn't it necessary to consult a professional in such matters. Surely a well John would agree with her decision.

"Maggie Pemberton," said the doctor.

Maggie stood up and crossed the half empty waiting room and walked through the door the doctor was holding open for her.

Then she followed him along a narrow corridor to his office, where he invited her to sit down.

Having sat down himself, he smiled warmly at her. "Now then, Mrs Pemberton, what can I do for you?"

Maggie had been a patient of Dr Barclay for nearly twelve years. He was a large, middle-aged Scotsman, with a kind smile, and a genuine concern for his patients. She always found him very approachable, but now she found it impossible to speak. Alison's phone call the day after the dinner had badly frightened her, and she feared for her husband's health.

Realizing that his patient was deeply troubled, Dr Barclay made an extra effort to put her at her ease. "Look, Mrs Pemberton, if something is troubling you it's better out than in. Talking about it won't make it worse, I promise you."

"Yes I am worried," said Maggie, "but not about me: it's John."

Dr Barclay was surprised. "So you're not here about yourself?"

Maggie shook her head.

"I see," said Dr Barclay thoughtfully. "However, before we proceed any further, I should remind you that John is also one of my patients, and I can't discuss him with you."

"I realize that," said Maggie. "Could I at least ask if he has been to see you lately about anything?"

Dr Barclay sighed. "I can't discuss that with you, Mrs Pemberton. Look, why don't you tell me what's going on and we can take it from there."

Five minutes later Maggie had told Dr Barclay everything; the words gushing from her at a furious rate.

"I can see why you would be worried," said Dr Barclay. "It's difficult to know what to do. It's up to John if he wants to come and see me. However, I sometimes run into him in the pub. Next time I do I'll have a discreet chat with him. How's that?"

Maggie smiled in relief. "Thank you, doctor. You won't tell him I spoke to you about it. He'll only get angry. He's so touchy these days."

"Don't worry, I won't. Now, how about you, are you eating and sleeping properly?"

Maggie laughed. "I'm fine, or at least I will be when John gets over this ridiculous vision of his."

Maggie heard the front door open and then slam shut.

The bang made her jump.

"Maggie? Maggie, where the devil are you?" John's voice called out.

Maggie waited in the kitchen, foreboding drying her mouth.

Suddenly her husband stormed in, his face pale with anger. "What have you been saying to Dr Barclay?" he demanded furiously. "He came up to me in the pub tonight asking all sorts of questions?"

Maggie opened her mouth to reply, but John wasn't waiting for an answer.

"Hee may be an excellent doctor but he didn't do much of a job keeping your secret. Within ten seconds I realized that you must have been to see him. So what did you tell him; that I'm having a midlife crisis or a breakdown; what?"

Maggie tried to keep her voice steady. "Of course not, John. You refused to go and see him and I was desperately worried about you. What was I supposed to do?"

"What did you tell him?" John repeated.

"Just that I was worried about you lately; nothing more."

"Then why did he ask me if my balance was as good as it used to be, and if I was having any trouble sleeping, or problems with my eyes?"

"I don't know," said Maggie. "Maybe that's the sort of information doctor's want to know about patients of retirement age."

"Not in the bloody pub they don't!" John shouted, his eyes wide and staring. "I felt a right fool. God knows who might have overheard."

"Dr Barclay definitely wouldn't have said anything if someone else could hear," Maggie protested.

"That's not the point," said John. "Anyway, that vision is something between you and me, understand. No one else has anything to do with it."

With that John strode from the kitchen, muttering to himself as he went.

Once again the front door was opened, then banged shut.

For a few moments Maggie stood alone in the kitchen, staring at nothing

Then a wave of despair flowed through her and she collapsed to the floor in tears.

CHAPTER SEVENTEEN

Saturday 3rd July

"Mmm; this is absolutely delicious, love" said John cutting off a second piece of meat from the Sirloin steak on his plate. "It's as good as Fillet."

"Half the price, too," said Maggie, who was sitting across the table from her husband. "George said he hangs it for at least three weeks before he sells it to his customers."

"You can certainly tell," said John. "No wonder he's always busy in that shop of his. Maybe if more butchers went to the same trouble as he does for their customers, the supermarkets wouldn't have such a detrimental effect on them. You can't beat quality, even if it does cost more."

"That's all right for you to say, dear," said Maggie, "but many people are on low incomes. They have no choice but to consider the price first."

"No one living in these times are so poor that they can't put a little aside for a piece of good steak," John replied. "You only have to visit the supermarkets to see the amount mothers spend on junk food for their children. Now when we were young it was a different matter. We couldn't even have butter every day."

"I suppose so," said Maggie. "Though it could depend on -"

John suddenly flinching froze the words in Maggie's throat. She put her knife and fork down. "What's the matter, dear?"

John, holding the fingers of his right hand tight against his forehead, winced and lowered his head. "Headache."

"Is it bad?" Maggie asked, becoming concerned. "Shall I get you a couple of paracetamol?"

John nodded.

Maggie quickly left the table and returned a minute later with two tablets and a glass of water.

Once he had taken them, Maggie guided him to the settee in the living-room.

His stiff, uncertain walk concerned her most of all, for she had never seen a headache bring on something like that before.

"You sit there and relax," she said as John lowered himself on to the settee.

He then leaned back and closed his eyes, pain creating a frown.

Maggie sat beside him. "Still bad?" she asked.

"I feel like I've been in a head-butting contest with one of those tough, mountain goats, and lost," John replied, keeping his eyes shut.

"Maybe it's a migraine," Maggie suggested. "They can be a lot worse than headaches. Anyway, see how it goes. If the pain hasn't eased in an hour, you can take another two tablets."

"Thanks, love, I'll be all right in a while," said John. "Sorry about the dinner."

"That's all right, dear. I can do you another steak later if you're feeling better."

Maggie then left her husband to rest and spent the next hour seeing to the dishes and cleaning the kitchen.

And when she finally returned to John she found him stretched out on the settee, fast asleep.

She smiled to herself. He was clearly free of pain, since his face look calmed and relaxed.

She decided to catch up on a book she had been neglecting, and settling into one of the two armchairs in the room, began reading.

Two hours later John sat up suddenly and vigorously scratched his head with both hands.

Then he yawned and looked at Maggie.

"How's the headache?" she inquired.

"Beaten into submission by the paracetamol, love," John quipped. "I could murder some tea."

"I can make you a sandwich if you like?" Maggie offered, relieved by his recovery.

"Just tea, love," said John. "Make it in one of those large mugs Jennifer gave us, and keep the kettle on standby. The inside of my mouth is as dry as the Gobi desert."

Five minutes later Maggie was back with the tea, but when John took the mug it slipped from his hand and tipped its contents on his lap before bouncing off his right knee and tumbling across the floor.

"Watch it!" he barked, jumping up and brushing furiously at the front of his trousers.

"I'll get some paper towel!" Maggie said, rushing to the kitchen.

When she returned and handed the roll to John, he snatched it from her, his face pale with anger.

"Just look at the state of my trousers!" he declared angrily, tearing off a few sheets and patting the large, wet stain.

"I'm sorry, dear," said Maggie. "I thought you were holding the handle."

"Well I wasn't!" John snapped. "You shouldn't have let go until I was. I could have scalded myself."

"I'll get you another pair of trousers and underpants," said Maggie. "You can change in the bathroom."

John didn't say anything when Maggie left the room.

She let out a sigh as she climbed the stairs. A perfect evening ruined, and she was certain that John had taken the mug from her before it fell.

The following afternoon a crash sent Maggie running into the kitchen.

She found John standing by the sink, staring at a puddle of water on the floor in front of him. Pieces of clear glass seemed to be everywhere.

"What happened?" she asked, getting a brush and pan from a small cupboard next to the cooker.

"I must have got water on the outside of the glass," John answered, his expression grave.

Then he stepped back to let Maggie clean up.

And as she did so, she noticed him flexing and unflexing his right hand.

"What's the matter with your hand, dear?" she asked. "Is it hurting? Is that why you dropped the glass?"

"I told you; the outside of the glass got wet," John growled. "I wish you would stop creating a fuss about nothing."

Maggie straightened up, but John walked out of the kitchen before she could respond.

Once she had finished cleaning up, Maggie joined John on the settee. She felt anxious.

John's face looked tight, as if the muscles were locked beneath his skin.

"Can I talk to you about something without it turning into an argument, dear?" Maggie asked.

John took his attention from the TV and looked at her. "What's that suppose to mean?" he said firmly. "So now you think we can't even have a conversation without arguing. When did that start?"

Maggie felt defensive, and tried to smile. "Well, you do get rather upset when I ask you certain questions."

John frowned. "Only when they are stupid ones, and only when you don't accept my answers and get on my nerves."

"All right then," said Maggie, "can we have a chat; just this once, without us falling out; even if I do get on your nerves, which I don't mean to?"

John was thoughtful for a moment; then he nodded.

"It's about your hand, dear," said Maggie.

John instantly looked at his right hand. "What about it?"

"Well, you do seem to be having trouble with it lately," said Maggie."

"I told you it's arthritis," John replied. "Just another sign of the relentless progress of aging."

"Are you sure it's arthritis?" Maggie pressed.

"What else could it be?"

"Well, maybe it's a trapped nerve in your neck. I believe it's a common problem. Alison said that -"

"Alison?" John cut in. "What has she got to do with it?"

Maggie saw his anger returning, but it was too late to back out. "She was only saying that she and -"

"Have you been talking to those two about me, behind my back?" John demanded.

"No; of course not!" Maggie shot back. "It's just that they noticed when they were here, and Pat wondered if you had a trapped nerve, so Alison thought she should give me a call, just in case we hadn't considered it."

"It's none of their blasted business!" John retorted. "And they can damn well stay away if all they do when they visit is watch how I eat."

"They were only trying to be helpful, John," said Maggie, feeling she should defend her sister and brother-in-law.

"People shouldn't offer help unless it's asked for," said John. "No wonder there's so much trouble in families these days; everyone thinking they know best."

Maggie said nothing more, realizing her husband was too angry to listen to reason.

CHAPTER EIGHTEEN

Thursday 15th July

"Jennifer, it's me, dear, mum."

"Hi, mum."

"Your father is ill, dear," said Maggie, her fingers tight on the receiver. "I'm terribly worried about him."

"What's wrong with him?" Jennifer asked.

"He's been having terrible headaches lately, and he keeps losing feeling in his right hand."

"Has he seen a doctor?"

"Yes. He was very angry when Dr Barclay approached him in the pub, but I finally managed to convince him to visit the surgery. Dr Barclay gave him an examination and then sent him to see a specialist."

"Did he go?"

"Yes, dear, last Monday. They gave him a CT scan."

"What are the results?"

"We have to see the specialist in the morning."

"What does Dr Barclay think?"

"He's not too worried at the moment because John hasn't any other symptoms. It could just be a trapped nerve and migraine, but Dr Barclay didn't want to take any chances. Sometimes very serious illnesses give very little indications that they are present."

"Mum, for heaven's sake, why didn't you tell me earlier?" Jennifer scolded suddenly. "You shouldn't be coping with this on your own."

"You're not supposed to know about it, dear. I promised your father I wouldn't tell anyone. Anyway, you know what he always says, parent-problems require parents-solutions."

"That's dad all right," Jennifer laughed. "But, look, mum, it's probably tension or migraine brought on by all this vision nonsense. When the scan shows nothing, he'll come to his senses; you'll see."

"You really think so, dear?"

"I'm positive of it, mum. So, stop worrying. Everything will be ok. Anyway, how are things between you?"

"Not too bad, I suppose. Although our conversations can get a bit heated occasionally. You know your father; he examines a worry from every angle before he decides to share it. And if he decides to ignore it, he expects everyone else to go along with his decision no matter how they feel."

"Is he worried?" said Jennifer.

"I suspect he is, dear. It's not in your father's nature to be grumpy, and he certainly has been that lately."

"I'm sure his mind will be put at rest once he's seen the specialist," said Jennifer. "After all, dad has the same frailties as the rest of us humans. Even Superman had Kryptonite to worry about."

Maggie laughed. "Don't tell him that for Heaven's sake, dear. He's big-headed enough as it is."

Jennifer laughed too. "Don't worry, mum, I won't. Mind you, I think he would look good with his underpants outside his trousers and a cape hanging from his neck. Perhaps he should audition for Grandad Superman, if Hollywood ever decides to make it."

"Oh, I wouldn't allow that, dear. I'd make a terrible Lois Lane. They would probably force me to go on a diet."

"Not a chance!" Jennifer declared. "A few extra pounds keeps the scraggy necks at bay. You'd be a fantastic Lois. Anyway, mum, got to go; lots to do: and let me know the results as soon as you can."

"Bye, dear," said Maggie. "I'll phone you tomorrow.

CHAPTER NINETEEN

Friday 16th July

Oncologist, Mr Andrew Rimkin stood up from his desk as John and Maggie were led by a nurse into his office in St Peter's Hospital. He had the false, cheery smile of someone used to welcoming people he was about to impart grave news to.

He said hello; shook hands with them, then gestured to the two empty chairs on the other side of his desk.

"Please, take a seat, Mr and Mrs Pemberton. My name is Andrew Rimkin. I am one of the Oncologists here at St Peters, and your case has been referred to me by Mr Harrison."

John and Maggie sat down on the uncomfortable wooden chairs.

Then the smile vanished from the Oncologist's face, to be replaced by a tightness of the lips.

Maggie noticed and her heart began to beat faster. She also wondered what an Oncologist was, and didn't like the sound of the name.

Mr Rimkin, a tall, lanky man with a full head of grey hair, and in his sixties, stared at his notes for a few moments. Then he looked at John through a pair of gold-plated bifocals, that sat on the end of his nose like a badge of wisdom.

"I'm afraid I have some rather bad news for you, Mr Pemberton. The scan has revealed a primary tumour deep within the tissue of your brain."

Maggie let out a gasp, but John stared stony-faced at the Oncologist.

"Cancer, I suppose?" said John.

"Almost certainly," said the Oncologist. "Although further tests will have to be carried out to discover the precise nature of the tumour, I'm afraid the prognosis is rather poor."

"You mean you're not one hundred percent certain that it is cancer?" Maggie asked, desperation driving her to hope. "Then it might be; what do you call it when it's not cancer?"

"Benign, Mrs Pemberton," said the Oncologist. Then he focused his attention on John once more. "Unfortunately, in this case it makes little difference whether it is malignant or not. You see, the tumour is situated in an inaccessible part of the brain, and as it continues to grow, it will eventually disrupt important neuron functions. Unfortunately, the surgery required to remove the tumour would be far too invasive. You would almost certainly be left paralysed and unable to speak. There is also the strong possibility you would not survive the surgery. And I have to say, Mr Pemberton, I'm rather surprised you haven't had other symptoms before now. The tumour is in quite an advanced state, and -"

"Could it cause hallucinations?" Maggie interrupted.

"You have had hallucinations?" the Oncologist asked John.

"My wife means, might I have them in the future?" John replied, trying to hide his anger at Maggie.

"We can't accurately predict the precise nature of all the symptoms you will suffer from, but yes, it is quite possible you might hallucinate from time to time as the tumour progresses. Now, I suggest that we have you in for further tests. That way we can -"

"How long do I have left?" John cut in.

"A few months, perhaps even six or seven; it's difficult to be precise in these matters," the Oncologist replied.

"Then thank you for your time, Mr Rimkin," John said, suddenly standing up.

He held out his hand and the Oncologist automatically took it, though looking surprised.

"I came here for a diagnosis and you have provided one," John continued. "Now, I have to be getting back home. My flowers need watering."

"But, Mr Pemberton," the oncologist protested as John and a stunned Maggie walked to the door, "there are a number of other options. Chemotherapy could prove successful in slowing the tumour, extending your life by a further six months, perhaps even a year if we are lucky and the therapy is aggressive enough?"

"No treatment, thank you," said John.

"You have to be monitored closely," said the Oncologist. "The headaches will probably get far worse. You will need medication and pain management."

"I'll take an aspirin," John replied.

"Mr Pemberton, you must reconsider," the Oncologist cried. "Your symptoms will be far worse without treatment."

But John was already closing the door behind him, pushing Maggie ahead of him.

"John; for God's sake!" Maggie exclaimed as they made their way across the hospital car park to their car. "You can't just walk out of his office like that. We have to find out what they can do."

John made no attempt to slow the fast pace he had set.

Maggie had to run to keep up.

"Please, John, stop for just a minute, will you."

John stopped and looked down into his wife's worried face. His eyes were alight with excitement. "It's begun, Maggie! The door to our new life is starting to open, and I'm ready to embrace it with every fibre of my being."

"Well I'm not!" Maggie cried, clutching at her husband's coat. "I'm not ready to lose you. There must be something they can do. You hear about new treatments being discovered all the time; stem-cells and all kinds of drugs. And the Internet; all sorts of breakthroughs in medicine are reported there."

John smiled and gently touched his wife's cheek. "I'm sorry, love, but I think the Internet won't quite cover this one. Sacred tumours are not exactly in its remit."

"What about the pain?" Maggie pleaded. "At least go back for the drugs they will give you for those terrible headaches."

John shook his head. "No pain killers, love; at least not at the moment. I have to keep a clear mind now."

Maggie became frantic. "But why? Are you determined to suffer? Are you determined to make me suffer, because that's what you're doing, John?"

"It won't be for long, love," John replied. "Anyway, there's pain in all good things; when you're born; when you're teething; going through puberty, or having an operation to make you better, or worst of all being rejected by someone you love but doesn't love you. Surely you're not saying that we shouldn't experience any of these things because they cause us pain?"

"It's not the same and you know it!" Maggie berated. "Those things are part of life; part of growing and learning. You're turning your back on treatment that could allow you to live longer."

"No I'm not!" John retorted. "Oh, why can't you understand, Maggie. I'm going to be reborn. I want to be reborn. And all it will take is a few months of discomfort. I thought you would be happy for me. I never thought you would get hysterical about it."

A hard glint appeared in Maggie's eyes. "Is that what you think this is; hysteria?" she said in a low voice.

John suddenly grabbed her arms, his face glowing with excitement. "Yes, but there's no need to get in such a state, love. In less than a year we will be young again, and just think, we'll have all that energy and colour back. I'm sick to death of being a grey person, a faded, washed-out image of my former self. I've lost all the colour in my body I once had, and I want it back again. I want to have the colour of the young again like I did all those years ago. Surely you want that too."

"You keep going on about colour!" Maggie cried. "The colour isn't a physical appearance thing, John, it's in how you think; in the quality of your life. And we have plenty of that in ours; at least we did before that horrible vision came along to take it away. Now, I know you have a brain tumour and it is something to worry about, but you must put your faith in God; in us. I mean, how many times have you heard about patients proving the doctors wrong when they gave them months to live and they are still alive years later. And another thing, they say the immune system can destroy all cancers. Maybe yours was weakened by that very bad dose of flu you had last year and the cancer started, but now that you are better it might be working on the tumour at this very moment; killing the cancer cells faster than they can grow. But you have to fight too, John. You have to give your immune system all the support you can by being positive and determined to beat the cancer, and you won't have to fight alone. I'll be there with you every minute of your treatment, fighting just as hard as you need to. But if you give up now, so will your immune system, and then I'll lose you, and if you really love me, John, you won't put me through something as terrible as watching you die."

Maggie suddenly felt a great tiredness that she had never felt before. It was as if the true effort in living was revealed to her, and she found that it was too great.

Her head lowered with fatigue, and as her husband headed for the car once more, she followed in silence, feeling as if she was carrying a very great weight upon her shoulders.

CHAPTER TWENTY

Saturday 17th July

"Oh God; a tumour!"

The words left Jennifer's lips as a biting chill passed through her body.

"That's what the Oncologist said, dear. John has an inoperable tumour."

Jennifer stared at her mother, looking for something in her eyes to say that she was lying. "But he can't be dying, mum! He just can't be. This is all because of some silly dream he had. You don't get tumours from dreams: it's impossible."

Maggie, sitting beside her daughter on the settee, put her arms around her and regretted coming around with such terrible news. But John had forbidden her to tell the rest of the family, so she couldn't invite them to their home. He said that they wouldn't understand, and would only make things difficult for him. Make things difficult for him; how typical of a man; how selfish! And what about her? Wouldn't the coming months as she watched the cancer tighten its grip on him, make things difficult for her? Had he thought about that?

Sobs from Jennifer brought Maggie back from her brooding. "Don't cry, dear," she said in a soothing voice. "We must be strong now if we are going to make your father see sense."

Jennifer pulled back from her mother. "But he won't listen, mum! Mark tried talking to him and all he succeeded in doing was to make him angry."

"Yes, dear, I know. And if I'm honest there have been times when I have wanted to slap his face and scream at him for what he's doing to us. But what good would it do. I have never seen your father so determined, so single-minded, as if this vision of his was the answer to all our desires, and it was his duty to go along with it no matter what our objections. Mind you, he used to be a bit stubborn when we were first going out. I'd want to see one film at the pictures, and he'd want to see another. And he would never back down, you know. No matter how much I pleaded, he just had to have his own way. And for quite some time I put up with it. But then one day we were trying to decide whether to spend a bank holiday with his parents or mine. I was willing to listen to his point of view, but was he willing to listen to mine; in a pig's eye he was. All he did was go on about how nice it would be for his parents to have us for the day. And when I mentioned anything about my parents, he'd say, 'yes, love, but you see -' How I hated those words. Anyway, we spent the day at his parents, of course, just like we did the previous four occasions. But shortly after that I managed to have my revenge."

Jennifer smiled, desperate to talk about something else besides visions and cancer. "So, what did you do, mum?"

Maggie smiled also. "Well, the following week, while we were alone in his parent's lounge, he got down on one knee and asked me to marry him. He looked so earnest and vulnerable that I nearly lost my nerve. But no, I had to make him realize that we were entering an equal partnership, and not some 'Me Jane, you Tarzan' arrangement. So, I looked him straight in the eye and said, 'yes, dear, but -' He frowned at me for a moment, and then said 'But what, love?'"

"And was he angry when he said it?" Jennifer asked excitedly.

"Furious!" Maggie laughed. "Oh, he tried to hide it by keeping his expression calm, but I could tell he was livid. You see, I never said those words to him before and I'm sure he suspected what I was going to do. Anyway, still looking him in the eye I said 'I'm very sorry, John, but I can't marry a man who only takes notice of his own opinions. And since you seem to desperately want to marry someone who agrees with you all the time, then you should marry yourself, and I hope you will both be very happy."

Jennifer's eyes gleamed with pleasure. "Excellent! And what did he do?"

"He didn't speak to me for a week; no phone calls, no letters, nothing. But when I wrote to him congratulating him on his marriage to himself, he gave me a call. And I must admit, we laughed about it for years afterwards."

"And you think you can change his mind about not having treatment?" Jennifer asked, hope rising within her.

"I'm going to have a damn good try!" Maggie declared fiercely. "Our lives together are an equal partnership and John Pemberton seems to have forgotten that. It's time he was reminded again."

CHAPTER TWENTY ONE

Monday 18th July

Maggie found the food on her plate tasteless, despite it being her favourite. The slices of ham were tender, the tomatoes sweet, and the lettuce was crisp, yet they had no flavour in her mouth. She looked across the table at John. His movements as he ate his lunch seemed mechanical, as if his thoughts were elsewhere.

"How is it, dear?" she inquired.

"Hmmm?" John threw her a puzzled look for an instant, then he understood what she had asked. "Oh, fine, love. Sorry, I was miles away."

"Where?"

The puzzlement was back. "What?"

"You said you were miles away," Maggie replied, "and I was wondering where?"

"It's just a figure of speech, love," John replied in a flat tone.

"Oh, but it was somewhere in this life, I take it?"

Irritation showed on John's face and he placed his knife and fork down carefully on his plate. "What's with all the questions, love? If there is something on your mind, then get to the point, will you. I'm in no mood for games."

"Very well," Maggie replied. "If you must know, I have been feeling something rather unpleasant these last few weeks; something I haven't felt since my first days at Boarding School when I was in my early Teens."

"What feeling are you talking about?" said John.

"Loneliness," Maggie replied, "a deep and raw sense of loneliness."

"All parents feel that," John offered, "something to do with an empty nest."

Maggie shook her head slowly. "No; it isn't that, John. The children left this particular nest a long time ago, and I have grown used to it. The loneliness I'm talking about is the one someone feels when they are living alone, with no one else for company."

"That's ridiculous!" John snapped, suddenly angry. "How can you feel alone? I'm here with you every day, for God's sake. Most wives would be glad to see the back of their husbands for most of the day so that they can relax and do whatever it is women do. Why do you think so many marriages are put under strain when the husband is made redundant?"

"Well, I'm obviously not like most women," said Maggie. "I enjoyed you being here, as a matter of fact."

John frowned. "Why are you using past tense? I'm still here, aren't I?"

"No, John, you're not," said Maggie, her expression firm, almost stern.

"What's that suppose to mean?" John demanded, realizing an argument was developing.

"I would have thought that my meaning was perfectly clear," said Maggie. "At one time the man I married was thinking about his family. No matter where he was, or what he was doing, a part of him was with his family. And this was always a comfort to me."

"And now?" John asked.

Maggie sighed. "Well, now he thinks only about himself. Every thought and every action is for him: a form of extreme selfishness, I suppose."

"How can you say such a terrible thing?" John cried. "I have never for one second ever forgotten my family? How can you say that I have?"

"When your so-called angel visited you that night, John, it was your subconscious telling you that what you have with us is not enough. That's why you have embraced this message from God, because, in reality, the message is really from you, and no one else. Oh, I believe you saw the angel; the tumour may have had something to do with that, but you're a good man, and you could never just come right out and say you are unhappy, living here in this house with me. So the angel came along to make it easier for you."

"Easier?" John shouted, his face hard with outrage. "I'm dying from a brain tumour; how can that be easier?"

"It's easier because it was the only way you could do it," Maggie countered. "But you could still prove me wrong, John. You could go back and see the specialist; or go to another one and find out if there is a new treatment out there."

John stared silently at his wife for a few moments, and when he then stood up, Maggie's heartbeat quickened.

"We've been through all this before, love," he said, "and the answer is still no. I'm not going to pass up this chance to be young again and it's not fair to ask me to."

Maggie opened her mouth to say something, but John was already leaving the kitchen with long, angry strides.

She threw her own cutlery on to the plate in sudden anger.

"You're a stubborn man, John Pemberton," she called after him, "a selfish, *stubborn man!*"

CHAPTER TWENTY TWO

Tuesday 20th July

Jennifer expertly guided the Volvo into the driveway of her house.

She switched off the engine and got out of the car, cursing the torrential rain that had made her drive home from the train station a nightmare, despite the windscreen wipers going full speed.

But as she made a dash for her front door, she was met with a disturbing discovery.

"Mum," she exclaimed, ducking beneath the open porch that did little to keep out the rain," what on Earth are you doing here?"

Maggie, sitting on a large, grey suitecase, stood up, her face pale and her eyes red. "I've left him, dear," she sobbed. "I have left your father for good."

Her mind in a turmoil, Jennifer opened the door and ushered her mother into the hallway, carrying her heavy case.

"How long have you been sitting out there?" Jennifer then scolded as she closed the door. "You must be soaked through."

"No, I'm all right, dear," Maggie replied, taking of her dark blue overcoat. "I haven't been waiting very long."

"You go on into the living-room and I'll make us both a hot drink," Jennifer ordered firmly. "I can't believe you didn't phone me at work. At least then I could have given you a lift from the station."

Maggie, detecting the annoyance in her daughter's voice, walked slowly towards the living-room without replying.

The last thing she was in the mood for was a row.

A few minutes later Jennifer sat beside her mother on the settee and handed her a mug of tea.

Maggie took a sip of the hot liquid and managed not to pull a face. As far as she was concerned there was a knack to making a good cup of tea, and although she had known for a long time that Jennifer didn't have it, it still always amazed her how awful the beverage could taste in the wrong hands.

"Now then," said Jennifer, having drank from her own mug, "why have you walked out on dad? You know he needs you?"

Jennifer's unsympathetic tone raised Maggie's hackles. "What about my needs?" she demanded. "Your father has become a very selfish man without a single thought for anyone else."

Jennifer stared at her mother for a few moments. Then she took a deep breath. "Ok; sorry, mum." she said evenly, "obviously I have made a judgement on the situation before knowing all the facts."

"You can say that again," Maggie replied, "and I certainly didn't come here to be judged whether or not you know all the facts, as you put it."

"Sorry, mum," said Jennifer. "I was just worried that you might have made a rash decision."

"Rash?" Maggie cried. "If anyone is being rash it's your father. I'm not the one refusing to go back to the hospital, and I'm not the one driving my family to distraction with talk of angels and reincarnation, so how can anything I do regarding your father be rash?"

"Look, mum," Jennifer pleaded, "can we start again. Obviously something drove you out of your home, so come on; tell me what it was?"

Maggie took a moment to calm herself. Then she smiled sheepishly. "I'm sorry, dear, I didn't mean to behave like this. It's not your fault, but I seem to be taking it out on you all the same."

Jennifer smiled warmly and touched her mother's hand. "Don't worry about it, mum. Take it out on me as much as you like. Would-be barristers have to develop a skin as tough as a rhino's if they're going to survive the mud-slinging that goes on in the courts, so it will be good practice. Now; come on; what has dad done this time?"

"Nothing he hasn't been doing since this vision of his started," said Maggie, the skin around her mouth tight. "We had a row, and I decided I just couldn't take it any longer. No matter what I say, he tries to convince me it's for the best; it's what I really want but haven't the courage to go for it."

"Is it what you really want, mum?" Jennifer asked, scrutinizing her mother's face for even a hint of doubt to reveal itself.

"No it is not!" Maggie shot back, squaring her shoulders. "I have always believed that we are allowed only one life on this Earth: that's why we are expected to make the most of it; to be kind to others and strive to be good people, despite all the temptations to allow greed and selfishness into our lives. All right, I would be lying if I said I didn't understand why your father has found his vision so attractive, after all, who wouldn't want to have their youth back. But it can only be a dream, not a desire that you would actually strive for. That's the thing that convinces me your father is completely wrong about this. We both have had a very good life, better than most I would say, and to want it all over again would just be selfish. Anyway, the world would soon fill up if old people didn't make way for the young and it would be spoilt for everyone."

Jennifer smiled. "Some people would argue that it is full already. Maybe God has been sending too many angels."

Maggie didn't smile in return. Instead she sighed. "Oh, I don't know any more, dear. Perhaps your father is right. Perhaps we should grab everything that's on offer."

"You sitting on my doorstep proves you don't believe that," said Jennifer. "So, how did dad react when you told him you were moving in here?"

Maggie suddenly looked guilty. "I'm afraid he doesn't know. I mean he does now because I left him a note, but I just couldn't face him so I left while he was at the supermarket."

The door bell ringing followed by fierce pounding made both women jump.

"I suppose that will be your father," said Maggie grimly. "You had better let him in before your neighbours call the police."

Jennifer left her seat and made her way out into the hall.

Maggie heard her unlock the door and listened as an argument immediately developed.

Concerned, she stood up, but her husband came striding into the living-room before she had taken a single step.

John came to a halt when he saw her.

Maggie was shocked by the deathly pallor of his face and the unkempt state of his hair.

"What's all this nonsense about, Maggie?" he demanded. "I come home to find the house empty and a ridiculous note on the table about you moving in here."

Maggie squared her shoulders despite an almost overpowering desire to wilt before her angry husband. "You may think the note is ridiculous, John," she replied firmly, "but it does convey my feelings about the way you have been treating your family lately. Now, Jennifer has been good enough to let me move in with her until you come to your senses, so you can rant and rave all you like. This is going to be my home until you stop trying to tear your family apart."

Jennifer slipping quietly past her father to stand next to her mother drew John's anger.

"You knew about this, didn't you?" he barked.

Jennifer matched her father's glare with a determined one of her own.

"As a matter of fact, dad, I didn't until I found mum waiting on my door step when I came home from work," she replied. "But that doesn't matter. I love you both equally, but I am with mum all the way. You have no right to disregard her feelings and just take it into your head to die. When you got married, didn't you vow to honour in sickness and in health, and in my books honouring is doing everything you possibly can to make the other person happy. And what have you done, dad, almost driven her out of her mind with stress and worry, and for what, some vision that any normal, healthy person would realize is caused by the tumour in their head. But you're not healthy, dad: the tumour has affected your mind; caused you to hallucinate, but you must be very sick indeed, dad, because not only will you not entertain the idea that you are wrong about this, you're even trying to involve mum in your madness: well, not while I'm around to stop you. Mum can stay here as long as she likes, and if you want her back you know what to do: make an appointment with the hospital to discuss any options you might have."

John continued to glare at his daughter for a moment, his expression unchanging. Then a short, grunting laugh shot from him. "My daughter the barrister," he declared scathingly. "Well, let me tell you something, love, you may be a bright spark in that firm of yours, but when it comes to relationships all your schooling so far doesn't add up to one hour of real experience. Your mother and I have been married for forty years. We know one another inside out. If my breathing changes for more than a few seconds during the night, she wakes up. If she turns over in the bed just one more than normal, I always ask her about it the next morning. She knows how I like my tea, how brown I like my toast, how level the sugar must be on the spoon, my favourite TV programmes, the films I like and hate. And I know her favourite colour, what material she likes on her blouses and her skirts, how she loves chocolate digestives when she's watching a western, but custard creams when the film is a love story. I know exactly what will make her laugh, cry, shout, nag, what will make her hug things or throw them. So when you have been married as long as I have and learned all those things about Peter, and a thousand things more, then you can judge me. But until then, mind your own damn business, love, because this is between me and your mother."

"Well, my mother has come to me for my support," Jennifer countered, "and are you saying I shouldn't give it to her?"

Caught off guard by the question, John stuttered a few unintelligible words, then he fell silent.

Seeing his confusion, Jennifer's heart went out to him. "Oh look, dad," she said in a soft, pleading voice, "I'm only trying to help. If you could just -"

"You're not helping; can't you see that?" John interrupted, his anger back. "You're making things worse. Can't you understand that an offer like this has at least to be seriously considered; not instantly decided on by a gut reaction. Yes, I realize that it will bring changes for everyone, but so does dying in the conventional way. And if anything, Jennifer, you should be glad that this has come along. I mean, your mother and I are in our sixties, the autumn of our lives, and how much time do we have left, five years, ten, or maybe fifteen if we are lucky. But with this offer we can have another thirty or forty years; surely you want that for us, don't you?"

"I -" Words failed Jennifer. Her father had just done to her what she had done to him. What was she to do?

"Don't let him use emotional blackmail on you, Jennifer!" Maggie warned, glaring at her husband. "As he says this is between him and me. My decision is every bit as valid as his, and since he won't even consider changing his mind, he can hardly do anything but accept that I can be that stubborn too."

Maggie then put her right arm around her daughter's shoulders, but kept her gaze on her husband.

"So; you're staying here, are you," said John, his voice low and his hands clenched. "The most important event in my life is taking place and you don't want to be at my side. Well, all I can say is that I hope you don't look back on this day with regret, love, I really do, because if there was anything wrong in my acceptance of this wonderful gift, I doubt very much God would have offered it."

Maggie's shoulders went back and her head raised defiantly. "I have had a great deal of regrets in the past few weeks, John, and I suppose I will be able to cope with one more. And I would have thought that in the list of most important things in your life the two of us getting married and the birth of our three children, and two grandchildren would have pushed anything else into at least tenth place."

John instantly turned and marched out of the room.

Seconds later the front door slammed.

CHAPTER TWENTY THREE

Monday 26th July

Six days had passed since Maggie moved in with Jennifer. But if she thought her actions would force her husband to reconsider his decision of not accepting treatment, she was wrong. Not only did he remain steadfast, he did nothing at all to try and coax her back.

His stubbornness made her want to scream, but she knew in her heart nothing was going to work, and that left her with only two options; leave him alone in their house, coping by himself with any attacks that may come upon him, or be at his side to help him over them.

When Jennifer arrived home that evening, Maggie's packed suitcase was standing by the settee.

"Mum; what on Earth are you doing?" she asked, taking off her coat.

Maggie, sitting on the settee, looking drawn, gave a thin smile. "I'm going back to him, dear. I should never have left in the first place; especially in his condition."

"No; you can't!" Jennifer exclaimed, rushing to sit next to her mother. "You mustn't back down now. Give him a few more days and he'll come round; I promise he will."

"I don't think so, dear," Maggie offered in a low voice. "I have been here almost a week now and he hasn't phoned me once."

"That's because you phoned him!" Jennifer protested. "I told you not to. How can he feel cut off and alone if you keep in touch?"

"Is that what you want him to be," said Maggie, "cut off and alone?"

An exasperated sigh left Jennifer. "No; well yes, but only to bring him to his senses. He's the one who started all this nonsense; why should you be the only one to suffer."

"This isn't about equal rights, dear," Maggie admonished. "Marriage is about doing what's best, even if one partner ends up doing most of it. Oh, I know young people these days have quite a different outlook towards marriage, but your father and I are from the old school. We don't keep score of which of us is carrying the greater burden."

"I know all that," Jennifer replied, "but it doesn't give dad carte blanche to ride roughshod over your feelings the way he has. He must be made to realize that even if he is ill, he still has responsibilities."

"Well, my responsibilities are at your father's side, dear," said Maggie, standing up.

"But you can't give in now!" Jennifer cried, standing also. "He will see it as you changing your mind about that damn vision of his."

"I'm sorry, dear but I have made up my mind," Maggie said firmly. "Now, I don't want an argument over it. I have to save my energy for when I get home. I'm sure your father is still very angry with me."

"Mom; you can't!"

"Now, you listen to me," Maggie announced. "That suitcase has been packed and ready since eleven-o-clock this morning. I could have left then, but I thought it only fair that I waited until you came home, so I could explain my decision. My husband needs me, so you can give me a lift, or shall I call a taxi?"

For a few seconds Jennifer stared defiantly back at her mother. Then she let out a long sigh and her stiff shoulders dropped. "Oh, all right, but if he doesn't start putting you first, I'm coming right round and have it out with him."

"Yes, dear," said Maggie, smiling fondly at her daughter. "Wouldn't that be a sight to see. I don't know which of you would win, you are both so stubborn."

Jennifer smiled too. "Like father like daughter, mum. What do you expect. Now, you wait here while I have a quick change of clothes. I was sitting right next to some yob on the train who refused to put out his cigarette. My clothes stink of smoke."

CHAPTER TWENTY FOUR

Thursday 26th August

Maggie opened her eyes with a start. She sensed something was wrong: there was no heat radiating from John's side of the bed.

Concerned, she turned her head and saw that he wasn't there.

She sat up and pulling back the duvet, slipped out of the bed.

The en suite bathroom door was open and the light was on.

"John?" she called out as she crossed the room. "Are you all right, dear?"

There was no reply.

Fear spurted in her belly and she rushed into the bathroom.

There was a crumpled figure on the floor in front of the wash basin.

"John, oh my God!" Maggie screamed, dropping to his side.

With trembling fingers she touched his cold face.

Then she heard slow breathing.

Begging God not to take her husband, she dashed to the bedside phone and called an ambulance.

Then she was flying down the stairs and along the hall to the front door.

A powerful blast of damp, night air hit her in the face when she opened it.

The shock made her gasp.

She had no idea how long the ambulance would take on such a night, and she begged God not to allow any hindrance to their progress.

Then she remembered John and she ran up the stairs and grabbed his dressing gown before going into the bathroom.

She lay the gown over his body. Then she sat down beside him, stroking his hair and praying as she had never prayed before.

Jennifer and Peter were the first to arrive in the hospital waiting room.

Maggie, sitting at the end of a row of chairs, burst into tears as they approached her.

Jennifer sat down beside her and hugged her tightly. "How is he, mum?" she asked in a strained voice.

Through her tears Maggie answered in broken sentences. "I don't know. They're examining him now. They think he may have had a stroke."

"Was it caused by the tumour?" Jennifer asked, controlling her emotions for her mother's sake.

Maggie wiped her eyes with a tissue. "They can't say for certain because of his age, but they think it might be because it was in the same part of the brain."

"Look, mum," said Jennifer, "try not to worry: he'll pull through. Nothing so small as a stroke can keep dad down for long. Lots of people survive them these days."

Maggie gave her daughter a haunted look. "But they don't often survive brain cancer; do they, dear?"

Jennifer could find no words to reply and looked imploringly at her husband.

Peter, just as pale as his wife, squeezed her hand in a silent gesture of support.

The Colour of the Young

Mark and Robert came rushing along the corridor half an hour later, just as a doctor and a nurse came through a door and approached Maggie.

The time was 3am.

Everyone stood up.

The doctor's expression was serious. "I'm afraid your husband is very poorly, Mrs Pemberton," he said in a soft voice. "There is still some bleeding going on, and we considered operating to try and stop it. However, because of the further complications caused by his other illness, there would be little point, I'm afraid."

"Is he conscious, doctor?" Jennifer asked as Maggie's expression became blank

"Yes, but he is extremely weak and you must prepare yourselves for the worst. However, he is in no discomfort, I'm happy to say."

"Can we see him?"

The doctor hesitated before answering. "I would prefer it if just one of you saw him for now. He must not be placed under any stress, but a short visit shouldn't do any harm."

"Want me to go, mum?" Jennifer offered.

Maggie suddenly straightened her shoulders and her expression changed to grim determination. "It was just the two of us at the beginning of our lives together, dear," she announced firmly, "and it is only right that it should be that way at the end of it."

"Nurse will take you in," said the doctor.

The first pleasant surprise for Maggie as she walked slowly towards the only bed in the small room, was the lack of equipment around the bed. She had so often seen seriously ill patents in medical soaps submerged in a tangle of drips, plastic tubes and bleeping machines. But except for one small monitor that did bleep, the area around the bed was clear.

The second pleasant surprise was to see John smiling at her, though he was lying flat with just his head and shoulders raised by two pillows.

"Hello, love," he said in a weak voice.

Maggie gave a cry and rushed to him.

"Oh, John!" she sobbed, frantically kissing him and stroking his hair.

The nurse placed a chair behind her and told her to sit down.

"Just push that button hanging next to you if you need anything, Mrs Pemberton," the nurse then added before leaving.

The head of the bed was also raised slightly and a single wire ran from a small sensor on the index finger of John's left hand to the monitor secured by brackets on the wall behind.

The regular bleeps from the machine, though gentle, were the most disturbing sounds Maggie had ever heard. She couldn't take her eyes off it.

John, looking very pale and drawn, noticed her anxiety about the machine.

"Not as good as the game consoles the grandchildren have, but watch this, love."

John's index finger then tapped the bed and the bleeps increased in response.

"I've been trying to get it to play chopsticks, but no luck so far."

Maggie knew her husband was making a supreme effort to allay her fears. "Don't do that, dear," she scolded, "you'll have the nurses in a panic."

The Colour of the Young

Suddenly John's eyes closed and fear jolted through Maggie.

Then his eyes were open again and he was smiling. "Sorry about that, love, feeling a bit tired."

"Are you in any pain, dear?" said Maggie, too distressed to feel much relief.

"No, love. In fact I feel rather good for someone who has a brain tumour and just had a stroke. This dying business is completely overrated, in my opinion."

"Don't talk like that!" Maggie begged, her eyes filling with tears once more.

The smile was still on John's face but it had a washed-out look about it. "Sorry, love, I suppose to you I'm not taking all this very seriously, but how can I when it's what I want. I just can't pretend that it's tragic in some way. God has made me an offer; a very good offer, and I accepted it. Maybe lots of people; the lucky ones, die knowing that they are going to be reborn. I mean, haven't you often wondered how so many people seem to be brave, even contented when they are dying. Maybe it's because they have nothing to fear, and they are contented because in no time at all they will be young again."

"But if that's true," said Maggie, "why haven't we heard about it before? Why aren't there parents walking around this minute, younger than their children? I'm sure someone would have noticed?"

A small frown formed on John's forehead. "What are you trying to tell me, love, that I'm not going to be reborn; that I'm going to just die?"

Alarm surged in Maggie's chest when the bleeps increased. "You already know that I find it hard to accept, John.? We discussed it often enough?"

"Not when I was in a hospital bed, we didn't!" John snapped, and the bleeps increased further.

Maggie reached out and stroked her husband's hair. "Please, dear, let's not argue over it. You mustn't get upset. The doctor said you need to get plenty of rest."

"So why are you in here trying to frighten me?" John demanded, his expression like stone.

"Oh no; no, I'm not trying to frighten you, dear: don't think that!" Maggie pleaded. "I may not be convinced that we are reborn into this life, but I do believe in God, and that we will all see each other in heaven when our time comes, if we have lived our lives as good people. I'm a Christian, dear; I have been brought up to believe that God looks after us in the way the Bible says he does. It's very hard to suddenly think differently when I haven't had the visions you had."

"But I don't want to go to heaven yet!" John protested. "I want to have the life back I used to have. Can't you understand that?"

Silence then reigned between them.

And when Maggie heard the rapid bleeps finally returning to a more natural rate she smiled at her husband. "Of course I understand, dear, and who knows; perhaps it is exactly how you say it is. After all, there are no experts on what is in God's mind and what happens after we pass on. Not even the Pope has those kind of answers. We can only have faith and believe in our destiny."

The warmth returned to John's expression. "You know something, love, you missed your calling. You should have been a philosopher."

"Heavens," Maggie exclaimed in surprise, "and spend my life asking questions that quite obviously have no answers; no thank you very much!"

John suddenly grabbed Maggie's hand, urgency and desperation in his manner, but the grip was nevertheless weak. His head also lifted and his eyes transfixed his wife. "Listen to me, love," he said earnestly, "you will follow me, won't you?"

"Of course I will, dear," Maggie replied automatically. "But I don't know how far in the future that will -"

"No; not in your own time!" John interrupted, his anger returning. "I mean soon, when the opportunity presents itself. You won't keep me waiting for you?"

"How do you mean?" Maggie asked as exhaustion caused John to lose his grip, and his hand and head flopped on the bed.

"I mean, you will make the same decision I did, when the illness comes along?" John explained, his breathing laboured. "You won't fight it, will you, love? You won't delay it, because I'll be waiting for you."

A sigh of resignation left Maggie. "All right, dear, I won't fight it. But what if I don't get sick: what if I carry on for -?"

A humourless laugh from her husband interrupted Maggie.

"You needn't worry about that, love," said John, his voice weaker and calm. "When I accepted on your behalf, everything was set in motion. So don't worry too much about suffering. As I already told you, this dying malarkey is definitely overrated: nothing worse than a bad visit to the dentist."

"All right, dear," said Maggie. "I don't want to over-tax you so you get some sleep. I'll be right here when you wake up."

"You know, I think I will nod off for a little while, love," John replied, turning his head away from Maggie and closing his eyes. "But if I do sleep for any length of time, I want you to go home. You'll only wear yourself out sitting on that hard chair."

"I will, dear," said Maggie.

"Make sure you do, love," John replied in a voice just above a whisper, "or you'll be the one in this bed instead of me, and you know how fussy you are about mattresses. I swear this one has been padded with coconuts."

"You rest now, dear," said Maggie. "I'll ask them to find you a more comfortable bed."

Having sent her protesting family home for the night, Maggie watched over her sleeping husband for an hour, until her exhausted mind began to drift, and eventually her head drooped in sleep.

A short time later the sounds of an electronic alarm and running feet jolted her from that sleep.

CHAPTER TWENTY FIVE

Wednesday 29th September

Maggie sat on the side of the bed, her eyes red from crying.

But her tears were from joy as well as sorrow.

Beside her was a blue shoebox full of photographs dating back to when she was a little girl living in Clacton.

In her hand was a black-and-white photograph of her parents Maureen and James Middleton, taken on the occasion of their first wedding anniversary.

Clearly the photographer hadn't been a professional; the lack of overall balance in the picture was testimony to that. Nevertheless it was her favourite of her parents, because their smiles and sparkling eyes portrayed true happiness; just like the happiness she had once shared with her husband.

She sighed. It had been a month since John passed away; four, long weeks of crying, angry outbursts and grinding loneliness where every day was a terrible challenge to just keep going.

Everything about the house had changed; the warmth and comfort it used to offer when she and John came home from some outing; the sounds John made as he tapped away on the computer keyboard in his small study whilst she watched whatever old westerns the TV channels decided to broadcast, and never often enough as far as she was concerned; the lovely, reassuring warmth from his presence as he slept beside her in the bed; and the mischievous smile as he made some funny remark about her. All these things were gone now, like faded memories of a long lost time.

To her the house used to be an extension of themselves - John's framed certificate from his degree in mathmatics, hanging over the fireplace: her china cabinet next to the television, filled with little souvenirs, or *'Nickynackies'* as her husband used to call them, of holidays too numerous to remember: the Victorian pine bed that came from the servants quarters in Longleat, or so the salesman in Windsor had told them. Of course they hadn't believed the sales pitch, but they liked the salesman who had a cheeky smile, and they loved the bed so a price was agreed, minus any provenance value.

All these things had turned an empty building with four walls into a living thing, full of life, hope and joy. But now the heart had been ripped out of it and it had returned to what it was when they first moved in; a soulless place, mourning it's past.

The phone on the bedside table suddenly ringing made her jump. She wiped her eyes with a tissue and answered it.

"Hi, mum."

The voice on the other end of the line sounded wonderful.

"Hello, dear," Maggie said smiling.

"You haven't been crying again have you, mum?" said Jennifer, sounding concerned.

Maggie managed to laugh. "No, not really, dear. I've just been going through a few old photographs; that's all."

"Not a good idea, mum," said Jennifer authoratively. "That's the sort of thing you could do without at the moment, so put them away will you and come round for some lunch."

Maggie was uncertain. "Oh, I'm not sure I'll be good company just now, dear."

"I won't take no for an answer," Jennifer replied. "So get yourself ready: I'll be there as quick as I can."

Maggie put the receiver back, and despite her earlier reservation, found herself looking forward to seeing her daughter.

"Another cup of tea, mum?" Jennifer asked, standing up from beside her mother on the settee.

"No thank's, dear," said Maggie. "One's enough for me. Your father was the real tea-drinker. God know's where he put it all. You know, I decided to keep count of how many cups I made him in one day, because he always accused me of exaggeration."

Jennifer sat back down.

"So how many did he drink?" she asked when her mother seemed to lose herself in her thoughts.

"Oh, thirty-four, dear," Maggie replied.

"Thirty-four," Jennifer exclaimed, "in one day!"

Maggie nodded and smiled. "And that's not counting the ones he made himself, though those wouldn't have been many. He used to say that no one could make tea as good as me."

"But thirty-four, mum," said Jennifer. "So what did he say when you told him?"

"He said he was the one good at maths and that I made a mistake. He put the figure at sixteen and explained that I also neglected to allow for tea that went cold in the cup."

"Did he ever leave tea to go cold?"

"Yes he did, dear, once, and it was so unusual that I even mentioned it to him at the time."

Jennifer laughed. "Just like dad; anything to win an argument."

"Yes; just like him," said Maggie, sadness returning to her face.

Jennifer took her mother's hands in hers. Her expression was earnest. "Look, mum, why don't you move in here with us. Peter wouldn't mind; he even suggested it, and the kids will love having you around. But I warn you now, they'll probably wear you out playing games."

"Oh, it's lovely of you to ask, dear, "Maggie answered, "but you don't need me under your feet. You have your own family to look after and a high pressure job to deal with."

"Then you'll be able to give us a break by babysitting for us," Jennifer pressed.

"I can always come round and do that," said Maggie.

"Oh, come on, mum!" Jennifer exclaimed. "I don't want you in that great big house on your own. A place like that is designed for at least two people, not one, and it will be a weight off my mind, too."

Maggie smiled and pushed a few strands of her daughter's long hair back behind her right ear. "That great big house is the place your father and I chose to live out the rest of our lives. And just because John is no longer there is no reason to abandon it. I'll admit that at times it does feel very empty, but that's only to be expected after forty years together. And you know, dear, loneliness comes from the heart, not bricks and mortar. I would feel it even here, but don't you worry about me; I have my memories to keep me company and in time things will get better for me."

"But, mum, you -"

"Shush, dear," Maggie interrupted, her voice strong and firm. "I've made up my mind, and it is a credit to your father that he helped bring up such a caring daughter. Now, when you phoned me, didn't you say something about lunch, because you might like to know, dear, unlike your father, I can't live just on cups of tea."

CHAPTER TWENTY SIX

Sunday 10th October

A fierce, throbbing pain in her lower back forced Maggie awake.

She opened her eyes, gasping for breath and moaning in pain.

She tried to move away from the agony that was somehow restricting her breathing, but it held her whole body motionless in its powerful grip.

She lay still on the bed, trying to focus her mind on the cause of her suffering rather than how it made her feel. Why was the pain so bad? True she had been feeling occasional aches over the past few weeks, but she ignored them because they didn't last; the longest no more than a few minutes. Age brought wear-and-tear; there was nothing unusual about that.

But this was different. Whereas the previous pains had been minor, this was raging in its intensity. It was radiating outwards from her spine, causing her body to respond with agony-driven spasms, erratic breathing, sweating, and an overall feeling of terrible weakness.

This time she was going to need help.

Accepting the extra suffering it brought, her left hand crept slowly towards the phone sitting on the bedside table. Fortunately she had always liked to sleep at the very edge of the mattress, and on her right side, otherwise the task would have been impossible. John used to laughingly tell her it was an emergency tactic in case of cystitis.

She grabbed the receiver and managed to punch in the number.

When she heard an answer, relief joined the pain. "Hello, dear, it's mum," she gasped.

"What's the matter, mum?" The question was desperate-sounding.

"It's all right, dear; nothing to panic about," said Maggie trying to sound calm.

"It's three-o-clock in the morning and you've just phoned me!" Jennifer exclaimed. "Of course there's something to panic about. What's happened? Have you had an accident?"

Maggie gave a very poor version of a laugh. "Nothing like that, dear. It's just that I'm not feeling very good and I was wondering if you could drop round for a while."

"You sound terrible," said Jennifer. "Have you got a pain: it's not your heart is it? I'm calling an ambulance right away, then I'm coming over. So don't worry, mum, you'll be all right."

"The only thing I'm worried about, dear, is that you're getting yourself into a panic just before you get into that car," Maggie protested.

"But, mum?"

"You listen to me, Jennifer; this is your mother speaking!" Maggie declared firmly. "Are you listening?"

"I'm listening," came the calm reply.

"Good," said Maggie. "Now, let's start this conversation again. I would like you to pay me a visit in the middle of the night, dear, because some wretched pain in my back is preventing me from getting out of the bed to get a drink or go to the bathroom. So there is no need for an ambulance or for you to break the speed limit on your way here; agreed?"

"Agreed," said Jennifer. "Is the pain very bad?"

Maggie managed another poor laugh. "Well, lets just say there are a few politicians I would like to inflict it on."

"God!" said Jennifer. "Ok, mum, I'm on my way and I'll be careful. The roads are probably empty so I shouldn't be long. Bye, mom."

"Bye, dear," said Maggie and she sighed for two reasons as she dropped the receiver on her stomach. The first was the ending of the very great physical effort required in talking to her daughter, and the second, the easing of her pain.

And as the pain diminished, her breathing settled to a normal rhythm, and the sweat evaporated from her body, leaving her feeling warm and dry.

She felt cautiously optimistic that her ordeal was over, at least for the night.

Half an hour later she heard someone running up the stairs and calling her name.

She frowned as Jennifer then charged into the bedroom and flew to her side.

And as Jennifer then stooped to kiss her, Maggie placed a raised finger between them.

"Stop right there, young lady!" she ordered. "You must have been going far too fast to get here so soon. I thought we had an understanding?"

"I didn't exceed the speed limit, mom; not once, even though I wanted to do a hundred miles an hour," Jennifer protested. "The roads were empty and so I managed to drive at the maximum speed allowed, all the way. And what did you expect me to do: you called me in the middle of the night to say you were sick, for Heaven's sake."

The finger lowered. "Very well, dear," Maggie said authoritatively, "you may kiss your mother now."

Jennifer laughed and kissed Maggie on the forehead. Then she sat on the tiny space that was avaliable.

"At least you sound a lot better, though you do look rather pale."

Maggie smiled, a good smile this time. "I am feeling much better, dear. The pain has gone for now."

Jennifer frowned. "For now? You mean you're expecting it to come back?"

Then suspicion showed in her expression. "You've had this before, haven't you, and don't lie to me?"

Maggie nodded and her smile vanished. "Yes, dear, I have had the pain a number of times lately."

Anger driven by fear put an edge to Jennifer's voice. "Why didn't you tell me?" she demanded.

"I didn't tell you, dear because there wasn't much to tell. The pains were mild; you know, just little spasms and tinglings that lasted only a few minutes. I put them down to age. After all, I'm no spring chicken, even if sixty is the new forty."

"So what happened tonight?" Jennifer asked.

Maggie gave a loud sigh. "I don't really know. I was fine before I went to sleep. Then I woke up in agony."

"And now?"

"Much better, but I do feel as if I'm recovering from a bad dose of flu."

"Then I'll give the emergency doctor a ring," said Jennifer, "just to be on the safe side."

"That won't be necessary," said Maggie. "Leave him for those who are really sick. There is one thing, though, you can do for me, dear."

"What's that, mum?"

Maggie smiled. "I would love a nice cup of tea."

Five minutes later, when Jennifer walked into the bedroom with two cups of tea, she was pleased to see that her mother had propped herself up with a couple of pillows.

"You're looking much better," she said, sitting down once more and handing her mother one of the cups with daises on it. "How's the back?"

Maggie took the cup. "Just a bit stiff, but no pain thank God."

"Well, you better not move about too much before a doctor examines you. It could be disc trouble and you might make it worse."

"I'll be careful, dear."

"Right then," said Jennifer, "I'll sleep in my old room tonight, and I'll leave all the doors open so I'll hear if you need anything."

"What about the children?" said Maggie.

"Peter will look after them. He knows I won't be back tonight, and if I have to stay on longer, we'll work something out."

"One night should be enough," said Maggie, taking a sip of tea. "I'm sure I will be all right tomorrow."

"I think we should let the doctor decide that in the morning," said Jennifer. Then she frowned and stared into her cup. "This tea isn't much cop; must be the teabags you're using, or the water. I'm surprised dad drank so much of it."

Maggie suppressed a snigger. Jennifer had a knack of bringing out the worst flavour even in the finest tea, but no one had the nerve to tell her. It was no wonder that Peter became a coffee drinker within a week of going out with her.

"Yes, dear," she replied, "must be the water or the teabags."

Jennifer walked into her mother's room at 9:30 that morning.

Maggie was just propping herself up.

Her sleep had been unbroken and she was grateful for it.

"I've given the surgery a call, and Dr Barclay will be around just after eleven," Jennifer explained. "And it seems you are to stay in bed until he arrives."

"What if I have to use the bathroom before then?" Maggie inquired.

"Thought of that," Jennifer announced, "and let's just say that horrible old wedding-present vase stuck in the cupboard for forty years has finally found a use."

"What if; you know?" said Maggie, embarrassed.

"Hmm," said Jennifer thoughtfully, putting her fingers to her lips. Then her expression brightened. "Dad had a miniature shovel somewhere, didn't he?"

"Jennifer!" Maggie cried in horror.

"Only kidding, mum, for Heaven's sake!" Jennifer laughed. "We'll cross that particular bridge when we come to it. Now; breakfast. What do you fancy?"

"Toast will be fine for me," said Maggie, having enjoyed the leg-pull, and delighted she was feeling well enough to. "Mind you, I think I fancy coffee this morning, if you don't mind, dear."

"Don't blame you," said Jennifer, pulling a sour face. "I'll get you some decent teabags from the shop before I go back home."

Dr Barclay frowned in concentration as he carefully probed Maggie's back with his fingers.

She was sitting up and leaning slightly forward. Jennifer was standing at the bottom of the bed, biting her bottom lip with concern.

"Could you lean very slowly to the left a little," said the doctor.

Maggie leaned.

"Now to the right."

Maggie leaned once more.

"Right, you can sit up straight now, Mrs Pemberton," said the doctor.

"So what do you think?" Jennifer asked.

Dr Barclay pursed his lips. "Well, as far as I can tell there doesn't appear to be any damage to the spine. From the severity of the pain she has described, I did wonder about osteoporosis, or even a slipped disc. However, I don't believe the problem is anything to do with the spine itself. It could be the muscles in the back, but again the nature of the pain suggests otherwise."

"Where does that leave us?" said Maggie.

"In the hospital for tests, I'm afraid," said the doctor. "If this had been a one-off episode I might have prescribed a few days rest in bed, before taking it further. However, since you have had problems with your back over the past few months, I think a scan would be advisable."

"But the others were only twinges?" Maggie protested.

Dr Barclay smiled. "Or warnings that last night was coming. Anyway, I'll arrange for an ambulance to collect you as soon as possible."

"I'm quite sure I can walk to a car," said Maggie indignantly.

"Until you have had that scan, I'm not taking any chances with you, Mrs Pemberton," the doctor replied

The Colour of the Young

firmly. "Now, you are not to move from that bed until the ambulance get's here, which should be within the next few hours; understand?"

"Oh, don't you worry, doctor," Jennifer declared when her mother refused to answer. "Even if she gets an itchy nose, I won't let her scratch it herself."

"Then I better be getting back to the surgery," said Dr Barclay. "I'll see myself out."

As the doctor finally closed the front door behind him, Maggie stared at her daughter.

"I think that man's a bully," she said, a smile making her statement a lie.

"Dr Barclay is quite right and you know it, mum," said Jennifer. "Anyway, you can't be sure you can even stand, not to mind walk, after an attack like that. There's obviously some underlying weakness there, so it's best not to take any chances."

"I suppose so," Maggie replied with a sigh. Then her face screwed up with irritation. "Oh bother!" she cried. "I was so looking forward to having my hair done today."

"You can have it done tomorrow," said Jennifer. Then a mischevious gleam appeared in her eyes. "Now, where can dad's minature spade be, I wonder?"

Only fast reflexes saved her from the pillow that was suddenly thrown two-handed from the bed.

CHAPTER TWENTY SEVEN

Friday 15th October

Maggie remembered the office from the time John had been given the terrible news about his tumour.

Now she was back without him, although this time she was less afraid. Yes, it was true that she used to have a fear of death, but that was probably a fear of leaving behind people she loved, rather than the actual dying process. But John was gone now, and perhaps waiting for her.

Once again an Oncologist, Mr Alan Higgs, was sitting at the other side of the desk, reading notes in a folder.

He was a good few years younger than Andrew Rimkin; perhaps thirty-five years of age, and he hadn't smiled when she entered, although he did shake hands and introduce himself.

Sitting in an uncomfortable chair once more, Maggie watched him reading and thought *'I wonder how long it will take you, dear, to learn that practiced smile, because your expression has already told me I have cancer.'*

As if in response, Mr Higgs looked up and presented what he believed to be a comforting expression.

"Now then, Mrs Pemberton, the results of the CT Scan has revealed that you have a small, primary tumour on your right kidney; malignant, I am sorry to say. And it is rather a fast-growing malignancy that has a tendency to spread rapidly to other organs. However, the good news is that I believe we have caught it just in time, and it can be treated successfully. There are no indications that the disease has spread. The treatment involves an operation to remove the kidney itself, but that won't have an adverse effect on the quality of your life. For as I am sure you already know, we are all fortunately born with a spare which can continue cleaning the blood to an acceptable standard."

The news wasn't a shock to Maggie, so she was ready with her questions.

"Will I have to have chemotherapy?"

"Due to the size and nature of the tumour, it is advisable. You see, although there are no signs of migration, it makes sense to assume that a few cancer cells just might have lodged themselves elsewhere, and the chemotherapy should mop them up nicely."

"What if I don't have the operation or chemotherapy?" Maggie asked.

The Oncologist frowned. "Then, Mrs Pemberton, the cancer will most certainly spread quickly to other organs and you will die. However, as I said, I am confident that after the appropriate treatment, you will make a full recovery. Now, I shall arrange for you to be admitted within the next few days. I don't want any delays in your case."

The Oncologist stood up and so did Maggie.

He offered his hand and Maggie took it.

"Try not to worry too much, Mrs Pemberton," he then said, a genuine smile on his face. "Cancer is not quite the monster it used to be, and you will be in very good hands."

"Thank you, Mr Higgs," Maggie replied.

Then she left the office, her expression one of calm acceptance.

CHAPTER TWENTY EIGHT

Saturday 16th October

"What about this one, mum," Jennifer suggested, holding a plain, cream-coloured cardigan with imitation mother-of-pearl buttons.

Maggie stood back and tilting her head, scrutinised the garment. "Mmm, I think I would prefer something with a bit more colour, dear: something more cheerful."

"Right you are," Jennifer replied cheerfully, putting the cardigan back on the rack. How she enjoyed these shopping trips with her mother, but it had to be said, she wasn't the easiest person to buy for. Invariably there was something wrong with whatever she chose, but she nevertheless enjoyed the challenge. Sooner or later her mother would agree to compromise, and then they could go to their favourite cafe in the high street for sandwiches and fresh cream cakes. For her it was a relaxing break from the high pressure of her job.

"What about this pale blue one," she offered, holding it at arm's length so that they could both study it.

"Much better," said Maggie, "but I don't think those large buttons go with it. Is there one with mother-of-pearl?"

"Nope," said Jennifer, "but don't worry; I have a plan. You keep watch while I snip the buttons of the cream one. I brought a scissors along, just in case this situation came up."

"Don't be silly, dear," Maggie replied, chuckling. "Anyway, I'm not that bad, am I?"

The Colour of the Young

A huge smile appeared on Jennifer's face. "Despite having to visit eleven shops and trying a hundred cardigans, course not, mum. Buying a gift for you couldn't be easier."

"Sorry, dear," Maggie replied, "it's just that nothing ever seems to be quite right. Your father used to say that shopping with me was like being lost; traipsing everywhere but getting nowhere. Anyway, I like this one the best, so I'll take it. I can live with those buttons."

Half an hour later, Maggie and Jennifer were seated at a small table in Sandra's Teashop. It was 12.45pm, and the place was filling with lunchtime customers.

Some came for the warm atmosphere created by a young woman called Sandra Harris, who was in the process of opening a second shop six hundred metres away in another part of the high street. Some came for the good food and reasonable prices, and some frequented the place because it was situated directly between a major bank and a building society. Sandra's Teashop offered excellent egg and bacon muffins which provided a filling breakfast for many a hungry member of staff of both establishments. And occasionally even members of the boards could be observed discussing high finance as they munched their way through hot, buttery fare.

"Two pots of tea, two ham and tomato sandwiches, and a selection of fresh cream cakes, please," Jennifer said to the young girl who was dressed in a black skirt, black shoes, and a white, frilly blouse.

"Doesn't she look pretty," Maggie offered as the waitress walked away. "You know, Lyons used to have lots of small tea houses like this one, furnished in the same art deco style. The waitresses were dressed something like that young girl, but I seem to remember the Lyon's girls also wore something on their heads."

"A bit old fashioned these days though, mum," said Jennifer.

"Perhaps, dear, but I was reading in the paper only the other day that clothes I wore when I was a teenager are all the rage at the moment," said Maggie. "Which just goes to show, quality never really goes out of fashion; it just goes into hibernation, that's all."

"Yes, mum," said Jennifer, smiling. Although she would never admit this to her peers, she had a fondness for early period fashions and etiquette, often imagining what it would be like to have a man see her to her seat before sitting himself, or opening a car door for her, or watching his language when he was in her company.

In surprisingly quick time their order arrived.

The tea came in two rose-pattern, china teapots, and the cups, saucers, tea-plates and cake-stand reflected the same, beautiful decoration.

"Shall I be mum, mum," Jennifer quipped, pouring tea into the two cups.

Maggie watched with a smile on her lips, but a frown on her forehead. How was she going to tell her daughter that she had just been diagnosed with cancer. She meant to do it when Jennifer called for her in the car, but it just didn't feel the right time.

Jennifer then poured milk into both cups and stirred them.

"Thank you, dear," said Maggie as Jennifer handed her a cup.

The Colour of the Young

She took a couple of sips and gave a sigh. "They always serve such good tea in this place. I wonder what brand it is?"

"You'll never find this particular tea anywhere else in the world, mum," Jennifer offered, having taken a couple of sips herself.

"You mean they have a brand all their own?" Maggie asked in surprise. "They must sell an awful lot to have that."

Jennifer grinned. "That's not what I meant, mum," she chided. "What I meant is that food and drink can taste better by their association with a particular environment. And since we both love this place, it follows that we enjoy everything associated with it."

"You mean, if I took this tea out on to the street, it would lose some of it's flavour?" Maggie teased.

"No," said Jennifer, laughing, "but you would probably be accused of trying to steal one of their expensive, china cups."

Maggie laughed too, and she began to eat her sandwich.

Thirty minutes later, the teapots, plates and cake stand were empty.

"That was lovely, dear," said Maggie. "Are you sure you won't let me pay half."

"My treat, mum," came the reply. "And now you can tell me the real reason for your invitation."

Maggie frowned. "I don't know what you mean, dear. We often have a day out together."

"Oh, come on, mum," Jennifer demanded, leaning forwards and lowering her voice. "I always invite you. This is the first time you invited me, and I know there must be something else behind it besides tea, sandwiches and cakes?"

Maggie's mouth opened and she let out a slow breath. She could no longer put off the bad news.

"Yes, dear," she said after a few moments. "As a matter of fact there is an ulterior motive for bringing you here."

"Thought so." The expression that then appeared on Jennifer's face told Maggie that her daughter suspected something serious was about to be revealed.

"Well, go on, mum," Jennifer prompted when her mother seemed to retreat into another state of mind.

"It's about my back problem," said Maggie. "I've been to see an Oncologist about it."

"An Oncologist?" said Jennifer, puzzled. "Isn't that a -?"

The sudden look of horror that distorted her daughter's features, tore at Maggie's heart, and she reached across the table and took her hand. "Please don't be upset, dear," she pleaded. "I have had a good life. I won't have any regrets if I don't pull through, except for leaving all of you behind, of course"

"Oh no, mum, you can't have that terrible disease!" Jennifer sobbed. "Not you too. I can't stand it."

Maggie watched as her daughter fumbled in her handbag for a tissue, and then wiped her eyes

"You must be strong now, dear," she offered.

"Surely they can do something for you?" Jennifer pleaded, her eyes looking haunted.

"As a matter of fact they can," said Maggie. "The cancer is only in one of my kidneys, and that can be removed safely."

Relief and joy dried Jennifer's eyes and she put the tissue back in her bag. "Oh, thank God. And why didn't you say so straight away: you gave me an awful fright?"

"Well, it's a little bit complicated," said Maggie, mentally bracing herself.

"I'm used to complicated," said Jennifer, sitting back in her seat. "You know, mum, I suspected something was wrong when you phoned me last night, but I never thought you were going to drop a bloody great bomb on me. Anyway, why did you wait until now to tell me you were that sick?"

Maggie shifted uncomfortably, and her heartbeat quickened. This was going to be hard, very hard indeed. "Oh, that was me being devious, I'm afraid," she answered evenly.

"Devious; how?" said Jennifer.

"Well; by manipulating you into being here when I told you."

Confusion replaced Jennifer's concern. "Yes; why did you do that?"

Maggie hesitated before answering. "Because; because I knew you would do your best to control your emotions when other people were about."

Jennifer jerked her head back, nonplussed. "What: you mean you wanted to control my reaction to you telling me you have cancer?" she declared incredulously.

Maggie's eyes lowered in shame. "That's right, dear. I know it was very cowardly of me, but I have a very good reason for doing so."

"This should be good," said Jennifer, resentment entering her voice.

And when Maggie's eyes met her daughter's once more, they were hard-looking with determination. "The cancer I have can be treated successfully, but I'm not going to have it."

Jennifer shook her head to clear her mind of shock. "What the hell are you talking about: of course you're going to have the treatment."

"It's what your father wanted," said Maggie. "I promised him before he died that I would do nothing to delay our reunion, and I intend to keep that promise."

Jennifer opened her mouth to protest, then became acutely aware that she was surrounded by strangers, and some were already showing interest.

Grabbing her handbag from the empty seat next to her, she stood up and glared down at her mother. "I'll wait for you in the car park, and you can bloody well pay the bill for this lot."

Before Maggie could protest, Jennifer marched out of the tea room, causing a few heads to turn.

CHAPTER TWENTY NINE

Sunday 17th October

"Don't just sit their staring into your drink, Mark!" Jennifer ordered, pacing up and down behind the settee in her living-room, wringing her hands with anger. "Tell her what she's doing is selfish and cruel and crazy and illegal!"

Sitting on the settee and wilting beneath his sister's fury, Mark tried to defend himself. "What do you think I've been doing for the past ten minutes, Jen! And as for it being illegal, I'm not sure that's strictly -"

"Tell her!"

Mark stared pleadingly at his mother who was staring back from an armchair. "Oh, come on, mum!" he begged. "You're not really serious about refusing medical treatment, are you? I mean, why would you? You're still a young woman with a good twenty or thirty years left?"

When his mother didn't reply, and Jennifer jabbed him in the back, Mark carried on. "Ok, mum, so dad told you not to have treatment for any serious illness that came along. But he had a brain tumour. He didn't know what he was saying. I mean, an angel; paying him a visit, and an angel no one else could see: these things just don't happen. Now, I think it's pretty obvious that his tumour had been growing for some time, before finally affecting him. And dad changed, didn't he. The morning after the vision he wasn't the same man: you said so yourself. Dad was always calm and steady. You could nearly always predict how he would react to anything, but once he had his vision, he became an angry and demanding person. He stopped drinking his ale;

got rid of his friends, and told you not to have any treatment if you got ill. That wasn't dad, mum, that was a very sick man who didn't know what he was doing or saying. Can't you see that?"

Maggie was stone-faced, looking as if she had never spoken and never would.

Mark received another dig in the back.

He turned his head and glared at his sister. "I'm doing my best, Jen!"

"Well it's not good enough!" Jennifer snapped.

"Badgering him won't help matters, Jen," offered Robert who was sitting next to Mark, and feeling lucky that his sister had focused on his brother, and not him.

"Why not!" Jennifer cried. "Nothing else is working. All you do is sit there as if were watching some soap on the TV. Why don't you contribute something instead of criticising my efforts. She's your mother too, you know."

"Be quiet, all of you!"

The authority in the voice made Jennifer, Mark, Peter and Robert look immediately at their Maggie.

"I have been sitting here for an hour, listening to all of you trying to force me to change my mind, and I have had enough of it," Maggie declared. "Though I must say, Jennifer, I am especially cross with you."

"Me?" Jennifer cried in disbelief.

"Yes you, dear. I had no idea that when you invited me around here, I would be walking into an inquisition."

"But, mum?" Jennifer protested.

"Be quiet, dear, your mother is speaking. Now, I am calling this family gathering an inquisition because that is precisely what it is. My daughter, my two sons; even my son-in-law are sitting in judgement, and I won't have it. For some reason you have taken it into your silly heads that because the four of you don't agree with me, you have the right to bombard me with both moral and emotional blackmail. And I have to say, Jennifer that you may be a rising star in your profession, but what I am doing is not illegal. It is not against the law to let nature take its course where ones own body is concerned. I didn't give myself this illness, but I have it now and I have the right to deal with it as I see fit."

"You know we're doing this because we don't want you to throw your life away, mum," Jennifer replied, close to tears. "What if it was one of us? Would you stand by and watch us dying from a disease that could be cured?"

"She's right, mum," said Peter, who was standing by the fireplace. "Dad was sick when he told you to do that, but you wouldn't allow us to. Didn't you try everything to convince him to go back to the hospital, even though there was no cure. You can't do this just because dad told you to."

"You all keep saying that your father told me," said Maggie. "Well, I loved him with all my heart, but this is something even he could never make me do. This is my life and it's my God-given right to decide how I should live it."

"It's suicide!" Jennifer cried. "It's a sin to take your own life, and you know it. No matter how you dress it up in rights and religion, the bottom line is that you are allowing yourself to die unnecessarily, and that is suicide"

Maggie gritted her teeth in defiance. "It is not suicide, Jennifer, it's letting nature take its course. I have done nothing whatsoever to bring on this cancer. I haven't smoked a single cigarette, not even when I was a teenager and all my friends were experimenting with them: the horrible, stinking smell was enough to make sure I never did. I have drunk only wine in moderation; I am only seven pounds heaver than I should be, and I have always been active. So if anyone is responsible for my cancer it's God himself, and if he has seen fit to inflict me with this disease I see no reason why he would condemn me for how I deal with it."

A loud sob burst from Jennifer and she ran from the room. Her thumping footsteps up the stairs dominated the silence she left behind her.

A door slamming shut put an end to that silence.

"I'll just pop up and see if she's all right," said Peter.

As soon as he had left, Robert gave Maggie a firm stare. "You're wrong about this, mum; you know that, don't you?"

"I know nothing of the sort, Robert," Maggie replied. "We see things differently, that's all."

"What about your grandchildren?" said Robert. "I saw on the news the other day, a married couple about yours and dad's age, who were killed while they were driving to see their family. And do you know what their daughter said when she was interviewed, mum, well, do you?"

Maggie shook her head.

"Then I'll tell you, mum, shall I. Their daughter said that although the death of her parents was something she will never get over, that wasn't the greatest tragedy for her. No, mum, she said that the greatest tragedy was that the children would grow up without really getting to know their grandparents. That's right, mum, that poor woman was thinking not about herself, but her children. Now, we couldn't do anything about dad. Oh, we came up with all kinds of ridiculous plans, but we didn't do anything in the end, because no real good would have come from all the stress it would have caused. Once we realized that dad wasn't becoming violent, we let him be. The doctors couldn't save him and neither could we. Now, I will admit that I have no idea at all what's going on inside your head, but the doctors believe they can cure you. And if you are just too selfish to put your family's peace of mind before your own, well, as you just said, it's your life and your right to conduct it how you think fit."

Robert then stood up and walked towards the hall. He stopped and turned back. "I hope you will at least take some notice of what your desperate family are saying to you, mum, I hope to God you do."

"What about you, Mark?" said Maggie when Robert had gone

"What about me?" Mark replied, subdued by his brother's words.

"Don't you have some sort of prepared speech, some words of wisdom and condemnation for me?"

"No one is condemning you, mum," Mark muttered, unable to meet his mother's eyes, "but how do you expect us to behave; just watch you throw your life away. And what if it was one of us, mum, would you accept our decision or would you remind us of our responsibilities; fight us tooth-and-nail to make us change our mind?"

Maggie's hard expression softened and she smiled lovingly at her son. "It would be quite different, dear. You are all still young, with a young family that must come first. So of course I would try and persuade you."

Mark stood up and smiled humourlessly back at his mother. "Well, mum, I think Rob and Jen have said it all. I'm not as clever as they are so I won't bother adding to it. It's your life, after all, but do you know what's going to stick in my mind for the rest of my life; a question; and that question will be, why did both my parents go insane at the beginning of a wonderful retirement?"

Maggie called his name as he then made to leave.

He stopped, his face grave and resigned-looking.

"One day, dear, when you are much older and bringing up a family is far behind you, I think you will understand my reasons for doing what I am."

"You know something, mum, " said Mark, "you never did give us a good reason for your decision, at least not one that made any kind of sense, so how could I ever understand."

And with those words he left, leaving Maggie to ponder on the reactions of her family.

CHAPTER THIRTY

Thursday 16th December

Jennifer walked through the long, hospital corridor towards Minster Ward.

The hospital smells were every bit as familiar to her as those in her own home, though far less welcoming.

'And why wouldn't they be,' she said to herself as her feet clopped their way along the hard floor. *'I've been here how many times in the past weeks; forty, forty-five, certainly more than the rest of the family put together. No wonder the place feels like a second home.'*

Then she was at the doors of the ward.

She ejected a soft, thick liquid onto her hands from a dispenser on the wall and rubbed them together. The pure alcohol instantly began to evaporate from her hands, and by the time she had pushed through the doors and into the ward, her hands were dry and felt silky clean.

A gentle tightness in her chest as she made her way past beds of sick people reminded her how much she feared and hated these visits, because they never brought good news, only news a little worse, a little more sad with each passing day.

A weak smile from her mother drove these negative emotions away; at least for the time being.

"Hello, dear," said the thin and frail lady in the bed.

"Hello, mum," said Jennifer, leaning over her mother and kissing her on the forehead.

Then she sat down on a chair and put a carrier bag containing bananas and peaches on the bedside table. Her mother hated grapes.

"You're looking very tired, dear," Maggie said in a soft voice. "You mustn't visit so often. Twice a day is far too much, and you are neglecting your family. Anyway, you're making me feel very guilty, you know. That poor lady in the bed opposite has had only three visits since I've been in here: why don't you say hello to her before you go. We have become friends, and she has commented on how lucky I am, what with you, Robert, Mark, Peter and the grandchildren traipsing in and out of here all the time."

"Try not to talk so much, mum," Jennifer protested. "You must save your strength. Now, I will say hello to; what's her name?"

"Agatha," said Maggie. "What a lovely, old-fashioned name. I don't suppose there are many Agatha's born these days."

"Right, I'll have a chat with Agatha, just as long as you stop worrying so much about other people," said Jennifer. "And as for the kids; they're certainly not being neglected. In fact I think Peter is spoiling them behind my back. Sometimes I wonder if he isn't one of them instead of my husband."

"Just like his father," Maggie replied. "I was the disciplinarian when you and the boys were growing up. We used to have so many arguments, your father and I, about what was an acceptable level of behaviour. When I forbade any of you to do something, you would answer 'But dad said we could.' Of course we never fell out over it really; opposites in a marriage is a good thing, in my opinion."

Jennifer smiled. "I think we did think of dad as one of us, now that you mention it."

"Yes, that's men all over, dear."

"Listen, mum," said Jennifer, suddenly looking uncomfortable, "can I ask you something?"

"Oh oh," said Maggie, smiling. "Your bottom lip is jutting out and that can only mean one thing."

"It is not!" Jennifer exclaimed, putting the fingers of her right hand to her mouth; horrified that she could have some quirky facial movement she didn't know about.

"Oh, it is dear; just like the second step down outside the back door."

"Mum!"

"It's all right, dear," said Maggie, "we all have them. Your father's eyebrows used to rise when he had a very important question to ask, and Robert tends to blink rapidly a few times. Mark, on the other hand, sniffs, as if he has a cold."

"So what do you do, mum, when you have a very important question to ask?"

Maggie looked away. "Your father was the only one who knew that, dear."

Then she looked at her daughter once more. "Now, ask your question."

"Well, it's about your reasons for refusing the treatment when there was still time?"

All humour left Maggie's gaunt face. "Haven't we argued enough about that already, dear. Why is it so important that you know the answer?"

"Because it is, mum!" Jennifer cried, trying to stifle the torrent of emotions that threatened to swamp her resolve to remain calm in front of her dying mother.

"You really want to know that bad, dear?" Maggie asked, her heart going out to her distraught daughter.

Jennifer nodded and wiped tears from her eyes.

Maggie sighed. "Then, I suppose it won't do any harm to tell you, and I certainly wouldn't want you to spend the rest of your life wondering about it."

"Rob and Mark would like to know too, mum," said Jennifer.

"I know they would, dear, but they found new mothers when they married; after all what is a wife if she isn't a mother as well, and I don't mean just to the children. Oh, I know they will ask themselves why I didn't have the treatment during a quiet moment, but there won't be many of those. Anyway, there is only enough room for one woman in a marriage; a wife will see to that."

"And what about me?" Jennifer asked.

Maggie's eyes had tears in them when she answered. "Daughters are different, dear. A young man will leave home to start a completely new family, whereas a young woman always extends her old one, and that's the real difference between the sexes, if you ask me."

"So what was it, mum?" Jennifer prompted.

Energy suddenly seemed to flow through Maggie. "You know, dear, you could say my decision not to have the treatment was made when your father and I were courting. You see he took me to a Michelin Star restaurant in London for my birthday, and it looked so posh I nearly didn't go in, I was that nervous. I imagined the snooty waiters sniggering at me behind my back when I picked up the wrong knife, or got confused by the strange food I was convinced John was going to order as a surprise. Anyway, I had nothing to worry about. The food he ordered was familiar enough, and everything was going great until John examined the wine list. Now, what you may not know about your father was that despite being a whisky drinker, he had a very good palate when it came to fine wine; red wine in particular. Anyway, your father looked at the list, and then ordered a seventeen year old bottle of Bordeaux. And it was very expensive, dear;

The Colour of the Young

fifteen pounds which was an awful lot of money in those days, but your father explained that courting was the most important period in a couple's relationship and should be celebrated in style and with no compromise. Anyway, holding the bottle in a white napkin the waiter poured a little into John's glass. Your father picked it up, held it under his nose, sniffed, tasted, then he looked at the waiter with that disapproving look of his.

'Is there something wrong, Monsieur?' said the waiter who was French himself; from Bordeaux for all we knew.

'Yes, there is, as a matter of fact!' John proclaimed, with his chin jutting out the way it did when he felt let down. *'May we have another bottle please. I'm afraid this one is unacceptable.'*

Anyway, a couple of minutes later the waiter was back with another bottle, not looking very happy at all. Once again he poured a little wine into a glass. John sniffed, and tasted and said. *'I'm very sorry, but this wine is totally unacceptable, as well. I would like to see the manager immediately.'*

So, there was I, dear, sitting in this very posh restaurant as John, the wine-waiter, the manager and even the chef sniffed, tasted and argued. They all tried to convince John that the wine was perfect, but he wouldn't have it. And just when I thought my embarrassment at your father's stubbornness in refusing to accept what the professionals were telling him, would send me running from the restaurant, one of the other diners approached."

Maggie paused, and there was a smile on her face.

"Oh, he was so distinguished, dear; tall, aristocratic-looking; a bit like Prince Philip when he was in his forties, though this man had raven-black hair, combed back tight on his head, and a small moustache. Anyway, in a strong, French accent he said *'May I be of assistance, gentlemen?'*

Then without waiting for an answer, he tasted some of the wine in John's glass, held the glass up to the light, sniffed it, stared at the label on the bottle and even closely examined the cork with a small magnifying glass from his pocket. Then he gave the both of us a bow and turned to the manager.

There wasn't a single sound in the restaurant as we waited for him to speak. So, the man, who only turned out to be one of the finest wine-makers in France and an ex-Michelin judge, said. *'Monsieur, your customer is quite correct. This bottle of wine has been adulterated with a inferior vintage; in my opinion a supermarket's own brand. And if you do not resolve this distasteful state of affairs immediately, you will be receiving an equally distasteful letter concerning your Michelin Star status in the culinary world. And my further advice to you, Monsieur is to treat your customers with the respect they deserve. After all, they are the life-blood of your restaurant, not mere chattel to be taken advantage of."*

Then having congratulated John on his palate and saying that there must be French genes somewhere in his family, he walked back to his table with the other diners cheering and clapping."

"What about your meal?" said Jennifer, delighted by the story. "Was it spoilt?"

"Not at all," Maggie replied, pleasure in her eyes. "In fact we were treated like royalty. We were told that we could order anything we liked and there would be no charge whatsoever. We were even given two bottles of their most expensive wine from their cellar: seventy pounds a bottle;

imagine! Of course to me there was nothing wrong with the Bordeaux, and the replacement wine didn't taste any better even if it was worth a month's salary. Of course your father was in ecstasy, but later complained to me that no wine he could afford would ever taste very good again."

"Did the restaurant lose it's Michelin Star?" Jennifer asked.

"No," said Maggie, "but the wine waiter and the cellar manager were both sacked the very next day. It seems they were using a syringe to extract the expensive wines from their bottles through the corks and substituting a cheaper vintage. They were doing quite well too; making nearly three hundred pounds a week, They got away with it because they only did it to customers who looked like they couldn't normally afford to dine out in such an expensive restaurant. But they certainly made a mistake with John. From that day I have rarely doubted your father."

"Good for him," said Jennifer, filled with pride, but the joy quickly left her. "Then you didn't have the treatment because dad was right about the wine,"

"Yes, dear," said Maggie with a contented sigh. "I knew you would understand. Now, it can get quite boring in here, so tell me what's going on in the world outside."

CHAPTER THIRTY ONE

Monday 20th December

There was a fine mist of rain falling as Jennifer stood next to her husband at the graveside.

The priest was carrying out the burial service in a solemn tone, and the fifty people present listened quietly, but feeling various degrees of emotions which depended on their relationship with Maggie Pemberton.

A few of the women, though total strangers to Jennifer, wept tears into small, white tissues and handkerchiefs. Whereas others were dry-eyed and expressionless; perhaps there simply to declare their respect for a former acquaintance.

Jennifer was pleased for her mother that so many people had attended. Far too often she had heard very sad stories of funerals attended by no more than a handful of mourners. At least her mother was clearly far too loved and respected to suffer that lonely passing.

Then the service was over, and after expressions of condolences and support were offered, Peter led Jennifer on the short walk towards the waiting cars.

"Excuse me?" said a voice from behind.

They stopped and turned around.

The speaker was a short woman in her early seventies, dressed rather colourfully in a dark red skirt, a white coat, pale blue blouse and brown shoes.

"I would just like to say how sorry I am about your mother, dear."

"Thank you," said Jennifer. "And you are?"

The Colour of the Young

"Oh, sorry, my name is Pat Roberts," said the woman giving a nervous laugh. "Your mother and I used to meet up at the hairdressers in the high street. We had many a long chat about all sorts of topics, and we had a lot in common too. Anyway, I was sorry when she suddenly stopped coming to the hairdressers, and I was terribly shocked when I read in the paper that she had died: cancer wasn't it?"

"Yes," said Jennifer.

"Such a shame," said the woman, "and if I can be indelicate, what kind of cancer was it; the newspaper didn't say?"

"Cancer of the kidney," Jennifer replied stiffly, wondering why she didn't like the woman.

"Such a shame, and detected too late, I suppose?"

"Yes," said Jennifer.

"Oh, such a great, great shame," the woman replied. "In this day and age, too. You know, dear, my husband had that very same condition; cancer in one of his kidneys, but he's right as rain now, worse luck."

An embarrassed laugh then shot from the woman. "Just my little joke, dear, take no notice. Anyway, if you don't mind me asking, was it both kidneys or just the one?"

Jennifer's eyes narrowed when a rush of anger passed through her. "In the end the cancer spread to her second kidney and other parts of her body: that's why she died."

"I see," said the woman, looking puzzled.

"I think we should be getting back to the house, Jen," Peter prompted.

"Why are you asking all these questions?" Jennifer demanded, now glaring at the woman.

The woman shifted uncomfortably as if she wanted to leave but something was keeping her there. "Oh, no particular reason, dear. It's just that -"

"Just that what?" Jennifer snapped.

"Well, dear, as I have already told you, your mother and I got to know one another quite well in that hairdressers, and in the few months before she stopped coming, well, I could see that she was ill. As a matter of fact she looked just like my husband when he had his cancer: you know, all drained, like."

"So?" said Jennifer, shrugging off Peter's sudden grip on her arm.

The woman stiffened her back with resolve. "So, I have to confess, dear that it seems strange to me that Maggie was too late to be treated. I mean, these days they can do wonders if cancer is caught early, and as I said, my husband had -"

"Are you a doctor?" Jennifer cut in, her voice rising.

A determined expression appeared on the woman's face. "No, I'm not a doctor, dear, but I do know what I saw, and when your mother first became ill, it wasn't too late. And another thing, she gave me the distinct impression that, well, that she wouldn't do anything about a serious illness if it came along. So, was that it? Did she deliberately refuse to have treatment? Because if so, I really would like to know why, if you don't mind, dear."

"Who said she didn't have treatment?" Jennifer demanded.

"Well, it didn't say anything about she having it in the paper," said the woman, "and you know what they are like, dear, they do love to get to the nitty-gritty of someone's suffering: extract every little morsel of the victim's battle for life. So naturally I assumed that she didn't. Are you saying that she did, dear, because she gave me the distinct impression that she -"

"It's none of your damn business whether she did or she didn't, you nosey old bitch!" Jennifer shouted in boiling anger.

"Well, there's no need to be so rude to someone who's only trying to offer some comfort," the woman declared indignantly. "I don't know, I really don't, you put yourself out and all you get in return is abuse, and I must say, dear, your poor mother would be very disappointed if she could see how you treat her very best friend. Clearly you don't have her good manners and breeding."

Jennifer opened her mouth to scream at the woman, but rage paralysed her vocal cords. Then her right hand raised high, her fingers in a fist and ready to smash the woman in the face.

"Right, that's it!" Peter growled, putting his arms around Jennifer. And as he guided her away, he looked over his shoulder at the woman who was staring white-faced at them, her mouth hanging open.

"Were you thinking of coming back to the house, Mrs Roberts?"

"Oh, ah, yes; as a matter of fact I was," the woman stammered.

"Don't!" said Peter. "You won't be welcome."

"How could she?" Jennifer cried in the back of the black Bentley as it rolled slowly out through the cemetery gates. "How could she speak to me like that? Mum wouldn't have had anything to do with that horrible woman."

"Course she wouldn't," said Peter, putting his arm around her shoulders. "She was probably one of those nuisance people you can't avoid. I'll bet mum cringed every time she saw her in the hairdressers."

"But she said they met there quite often?" said Jennifer. "They must have been friends?"

"No mystery to that," Peter replied. "I'll bet you anything that she had someone working in the hairdressers who fitted her in every time mum made an appointment."

Jennifer stared at her husband with red-stained eyes. "A stalker, you mean?"

Peter chuckled. "Hardly a stalker, love, just a sad old biddy living on gossip and innuendos. Now, forget her, you won't see her again. And if she does become a pest, I'll pay that husband of hers a visit and give him a right thump in the breadbasket, one kidney or not."

"But she was right about mum, wasn't she?" said Jennifer, feeling a little better.

Peter shook his head. "Don't worry, darling, a silly woman like that could never be right about Maggie Pemberton: she doesn't have the brains."

"I'm glad mum's buried beside dad," said Jennifer.

"That was your dad's doing," said Peter. "He realized there could be a problem with overcrowding years ago and did something about it. Now, you will soon have a house full of decent people: feel up to it?"

Jennifer nodded and smiled.

"That's my girl," said Peter, kissing her on the forehead.

EPILOGUE

Thursday 23rd December 2010

The pub was crowded, and if not for the smoking ban, the atmosphere would have been thick with smoke; a situation that used to keep Mary Harvey well away from such places.

But now pubs were as fresh as any place where human beings gathered into small places, could be, and so as she sat alone at a tiny, square table, in a corner of the public bar, she was contented, though a little nervous. Blind dates weren't her usual thing, but under some strange compulsion the previous week, she had joined a dating agency; but an agency who introduced mystery into the proceedings. As far as they were concerned, no one really had a type. They only thought they had, and the agency saw it as their duty to open the eyes of their clients to other possibilities. And for the ten years of their existence they had been very successful.

Mary wondered what her unknown date would be like and if he would be her type. These were the questions she frequently asked herself as she waited for him to arrive. However just as frequently she scolded herself for doing so. After all, what was her type: she couldn't say he had to be tall, because she had seen short men she would have dated. Hair colour, be it black, brown, blond, even bald; wasn't it true that if he was handsome anyway, it wouldn't matter. Then again he didn't have to be handsome so long as he had a nice personality; on the other hand, a little bad-boy behaviour always had a certain allure for her. 'Oh, stop it, Mary for Heaven's sake!' she silently scolded herself, wringing her hands under the table.

Then she picked up her glass of white wine and sipped from it.

Occasionally she saw some man give her a momentary look, but she considered that she wasn't attractive enough to hold those stares longer. For a start she was rather tall; five feet nine, with a thin, almost gangly appearance. Her black hair was wiry and defied all attempts to tame it, so there was always a few strands sticking out somewhere. Somehow clothes seemed not to like her, and even though she was dressed in a new pair of black slacks, black shoes with thick heels, and a cream blouse; all costing more than she could really afford, she still felt underdressed somehow. 'Huh, some catch you will be!' she said to herself.

"Mary?" said a hesitant voice that made her jump.

She looked up at the man who had appeared beside her. "Yes, I'm Mary Harvey."

A large smile warmed the man's serious expression.

He held out his hand. "Eddy Anderson; nice to meet you."

Mary nervously took his hand. "Nice to meet you, too."

The man then sat in the seat opposite. "Been waiting long?"

"A little while," Mary replied.

Eddy's large, blue eyes narrowed in alarm. "God, I'm not late, am I? I'm so sorry, I thought 8.30 was agreed by the agency. My watch must be slow."

"No, you're not late," Mary said hurriedly. "I thought I would get here early; you know, relax a little."

Eddy grinned. "Thought you'd check me out first and do a runner if I turned out to be Quasimodo's brother: don't blame you."

"No," Mary protested, "that's not it at all! I really did want time to relax."

"Well, there's no way you can be as tense as me," said Eddy. "Do you know something, Mary, I had to come in through those doors seven times, and each time I did I looked for you. And when I spotted you, well, I was so pleased I finally managed to overcome my nerves and approach you."

Mary began to relax. She liked this young man with his curly, brown hair, thin face and kind expression.

"So tell me about yourself; are you a local like me?" said Eddy. "Fantastic place, St Ives. No wonder artists arrive here in their hundreds each year, looking for that perfect sunset or whatever it is they're after. Mind you, I don't know very -"

Suddenly he stopped in embarrassment. "Sorry, I'm rambling; nerves, I'm afraid. Anyway, I really would like to know more about you, and I promise I won't ramble."

Mary shrugged. "There's not a great deal to tell really. I was brought up in St Ives and I'm now working for a stationary firm."

"What about family?" Eddy asked.

Mary's face clouded. "I don't have a family. I was brought up in an orphanage."

Eddy stiffened in surprise. "Not the one in Hillborne Street?"

Mary nodded. "Why, do you know it?"

A laugh shot from Eddy. *"Know it; you bet I do!* I was brought up there too."

Mary was just as surprised. "You're an orphan as well?" Then she frowned. "I don't remember seeing you there?"

"That could be due to the differences in our age. If you don't mind me asking, how old are you?"

"Twenty," said Mary.

"I'm twenty-five," said Eddy, "so you would have been about thirteen when I left. We should remember each other, I suppose, but for some reason my memory is a bit vague concerning that particular period of my life. Anyway, how did you get on there?"

Mary shrugged. "Not too bad. I remember that I was happy; at least I think I was: it's getting hard to remember lately."

Eddy smiled sympathetically. "I suppose no one want's to think about being brought up without parents, so your mind tries to erase it."

"I expect so," Mary agreed, looking sad. "I was thinking of paying them a visit to see if they have any information about when I first arrived there."

"Then all I can say is good luck," said Eddy, frowning.

"How do you mean?" Mary asked.

"Well, as a matter of fact I did just that last year. I had a couple of questions that were niggling away at me so I went back to find answers."

"And?" said Mary, eager to know.

Eddy spread his hands. "Everything had changed. The place had been taken over by new people, and would you believe they couldn't find any of my records."

"What happened to them?"

"They said they must have been lost when the old records were put on computer. Seems it does happen sometimes."

"Wouldn't the staff have remembered you?" Mary suggested.

"All new staff as well," said Eddy. "And, you know, although the outside of the building was familiar, I couldn't shake off this feeling that I had never been inside. I even had to ask directions to the different offices, and as far as I could tell, the whole building was very old, with no sign of any recent alterations."

"That's very strange," said Mary.

"Isn't it just," Eddy agreed.

"So what did you do then?" Mary asked.

Eddy smiled. "What did I do; I put it all behind me, of course. The orphanage is the past; only the future matters to me now."

Suddenly a warmth appeared in his eyes. "You know, Mary, although I have only just met you, I would very much like for you to be part of that future; if I haven't already put you right off me, that is?"

Mary felt a flush of embarrassment, but it was also a pleasant feeling.

"Oh, sorry," said Eddy sheepishly. "I'm rather impulsive these days. I just want to get on with things. I don't know why but life seems to be pulling at me constantly. I should try and curb it though."

"Why?" Mary asked, intrigued.

"Well, a few weeks ago I paid out three hundred pounds for a duck-feather duvet, just because it looked and felt fantastic."

"What's wrong with that," said Mary.

Eddy grinned. "Nothing, except I'm allergic to duck feathers."

"But you didn't know that at the time," Maggie offered.

"I'm afraid I did," Eddy replied, pulling a sheepish face.

Mary laughed. "I see what you mean about being impulsive."

"Didn't stop scratching for a week," said Eddy. "Anyway, this is supposed to be a date, so, can I get you a drink?"

Mary nodded.

"White wine?"

"Yes please."

"White wine it is," said Eddy standing up, "and whisky for me."

"Oh, not real ale?" said Mary, not sure why she was surprised.

Eddy looked alarmed. "God; you don't only date real ale drinkers, do you? I went out with someone who never dated cat owners, and since I do have a cat I knew there could be a problem. Of course when I invited her to my place, I made sure Tonto was off looking for females, but she spotted the scratches on the furniture and she was off too, looking for a cat-hating male, I suppose."

"Oh no, I'm nothing like that," said Mary. "I really don't know why I asked you such a ridiculous question; nerves, I guess."

Eddy visibly relaxed. "I only drink whisky; love the stuff as a matter of fact."

Then he balked. "God; don't worry, I don't have a drink problem, or anything like that: three drinks and that's me done. No; it's just that I can't seem to drink anything else."

"That's all right," said Mary. "We all have our favourites."

Eddy then stared at her for a moment, seemingly undecided about something.

"I'm quite happy to go Dutch," Mary offered, thinking Eddy might have money worries.

"No, that's not it," said Eddy. "It's just that I would like you to; oh; forget it. There's no way you would on a first date. You don't even know me."

"Why not ask and see," Mary prompted. "What wouldn't I do on a first date?"

"Well; go to the pictures with me. It's just that it's a remake of one of my favourite films, and it finishes at the cinema tonight."

"I'd love to go," said Mary.

"Fantastic!" Eddy declared. Then he frowned. "You don't mind it's a western, do you?"

Mary smiled. "I don't mind westerns at all."

"Fantastic!" Eddy repeated. "I suppose I'd better hurry up and get those drinks, then."

"I suppose you'd better," said Mary, laughing.

Eddy laughed too. "Right you are; *pardner.*"

The End